STARTING
FROM SCRATCH

STARTING FROM SCRATCH

•

Susan Ralph

AVALON BOOKS
NEW YORK

Published by Thomas Bouregy & Co., Inc.
160 Madison Avenue, New York, NY 10016

Library of Congress Cataloging-in-Publication Data

Ralph, Susan, 1938–
    Starting from scratch / Susan Ralph.
        p.   cm.
    ISBN 978-0-8034-7765-0
    1. Self-actualization (Psychology)—Fiction.   I. Title.
    PS3608.A6954S73   2010
    813'.6—dc22
                                              2009053847

PRINTED IN THE UNITED STATES OF AMERICA
ON ACID-FREE PAPER
BY HADDON CRAFTSMEN, BLOOMSBURG, PENNSYLVANIA

To Catherine Lynn, Allison Jane, Kristen Elizabeth, Edmund Hamilton, and Madelyn Kay.

Chapter One

Rain, dropped by a late afternoon thunderstorm, steamed on the hot pavement outside the windows of Jolly's Café. Inside, my fiancé was on the hot seat, and I was steaming.

The air-conditioning unit, stuck in the wall over my head, tried to justify its existence—clunking and blowing without a break. But, for all its sound and fury, it wasn't cooling off anything. Not the interior of Jolly's Café. Not me.

Humidity had curled Jake's hair into ringlets. His gym–toned muscles rippled beneath the taut fabric of his T-shirt. But Jake's physical assets weren't what had me steaming.

I'd asked a question.

And hadn't heard an answer.

I glared.

Jake's eyes rolled from side to side. His fingers

tapped a staccato beat on the table. He chewed his bottom lip.

"Ah . . . ," he uttered, and trained his gaze on his dinner plate, picked up a French fry and began dipping it in and out of a blob of catsup.

I continued glaring. This time I wasn't letting him off the hook until I got a satisfactory explanation.

But, expressing himself isn't one of Jake's strong points. For him to come up with a credible response would be difficult. But he was trying.

I could tell.

His lips were moving.

Seconds ticked by.

Jake shoved his plate away, leaving a large portion of his rib-eye steak uneaten.

Guilty.

I leaned back in the seat. "So—"

He looked at me with his endearing I-know-I've-been-bad expression, waiting for me to back down.

But this time I didn't plan to.

"—the answer is?"

"This isn't a game show like *Jeopardy,* Ags."

"Right. It's an interrogation. And the truth will set you free."

A shadow fell across the table. Jake *sighed,* shifted his gaze from his plate, and looked up at our waitress.

"Y'all want anything else?" Rita, Jolly's senior waitress, asked as she sat Jake's pie in front of him and re-filled our tea glasses.

I answered through gritted teeth, keeping my eyes on the doomed man. "Thanks, Rita. Everything's fine."

A loud "pfft" was Rita's response. She dropped our bill on the table, and moved on.

Jake smiled at me. My heart flipped several times. Maybe he was guilty of being innocent. My information about his two–timing me—for the third time—was secondhand—circumstantial evidence in a court of law.

Give me a reason to believe.

I repeated my question one more time—in case my informant had been wrong—in case Jake could prove he hadn't been cheating on me.

"Why were you with a blond hussy in the Culver City Diner two nights ago?"

Jake's fingers fumbled with the quarter he'd laid on the table when we sat down. He got hold of the coin and slipped it into the booth's jukebox selector. He took his sweet time flipping through the title cards before punching in the letter and number combinations for the songs he wanted to hear.

My foot tapped the table leg.

Instead of giving me an acceptable answer, Jake picked up his fork, cut off a chunk of his sweet potato pie and mumbled something about a flat tire.

The clatter of the air-conditioner swallowed the rest of his excuse. But, his exact words didn't matter. Whatever he'd come up with was a lie. And the truth was this man, the man I planned to spend the rest of my life with, was missing the faithful gene.

I sizzled. My strong alter ego, the one I call my inner Amazon, rose to the task, dousing my usual inclination to find a way to restore order—regardless of what restoring order cost me.

Jake had struck out. His inning was over. I could no longer pretend he would change from a low-down, two-timing louse into a decent guy I could trust.

"Ha," I said. I gathered my courage, slipped it over my shoulders like chain mail armor, and then slid across the bench seat. Free of the confinement of the booth, I faced the front edge of the table, took a balanced stance, and waved my Jolly's dull-edged dinner knife through the air like a sword.

Jake cut another forkful of sweet potato pie and lifted the loaded fork toward his mouth.

I tugged off my engagement ring—with a diamond so small someone with twenty/twenty vision had to squint to see it—and mashed the symbol of our commitment into the remainder of his orange–colored pie.

Jake sat back with his hands raised toward the ceiling in the universal sign of surrender.

"Ags . . . sit down," he said in a stage whisper. He smiled the crooked smile that always melted my heart. But this time, my inner Amazon blinded me to his charms. My heart remained frozen. I had no intention of honoring the white flag he waved.

With a sweep of my hand I knocked his dessert plate with its mushy contents into his lap. And then bit down hard on my bottom lip to keep from laughing at the look of stunned disbelief contorting his handsome face.

With my lips clamped tight—to prevent any revealing sounds like a sob from emerging—I spun a quarter turn and marched down the café's aisle to the strains of Elvis' rendition of "Blue Suede Shoes" blaring from the jukebox.

Customers, on the stools lining Jolly's counter, turned to watch my progress like the wedding guests in church pews turn to watch a bride hitch-step to the altar.

An experience I would never have. My dream of being a bride was over. Instead of hitching down a church aisle, carrying a bouquet of pink tulips tied with a silvery-pink ribbon, I was stomping down the aisle of a blue-plate special café, gripping the handle of a dinner knife with a smear of butter on the blade.

Halfway to the exit, my steps slowed, my heart quivered. My bottom lip mimicked the movement of my heart.

Don't stop. My inner Amazon shouted in my head. *Get out while you're still steamed.*

I forced my feet onward. Three-quarters of the way to the door, I tasted freedom. My stride lengthened. My chin lifted. Turning back, promising to wash and iron Jake's jeans and cleaning off the ring and putting it back on my finger, wasn't going to happen. Jake could do whatever he wanted, whenever he wanted, with whomever he wanted—I no longer cared.

The front door of the café slammed behind me. My feet flew down the steps. I changed songs, humming "Jailhouse Rock" as I half-walked, half-ran alongside the dark road in the direction of home. A chorus of croaking frogs, chirping crickets and flickering fireflies cheered me on.

The car headlights I'd expected to approach from behind didn't.

Sorrow replaced euphoria.

As I neared my grandmother's bright green house

with the pink shutters, the house I'd called home all of my life, I lost my bravado. My inner Amazon had dissolved in the dark. My normal mild-mannered, don't-make-waves persona was back in control.

I got myself the rest of the way home and sat on the top step of the front porch. Jake had probably taken the time to clean off the pie. He'd probably spent some time joking with the other male customers about the trouble with women. All of these things would have delayed his following me.

I wrapped my arms around my knees and rocked my upper body back and forth. When he showed up and begged forgiveness, could I abandon him after all of the years we'd been together?

I didn't know.

Jake took full advantage of my complacent and nurturing mother-hen personality. But so did everyone else. Jake had faults. I had faults. His cheating was hard to overlook. But maybe my roller-coaster emotions were hard for him to overlook.

Twenty minutes passed. Jake was not coming.

I considered my options.

Leave town, said a voice in my head.

Could I?

Minutes after I was born—as the story goes—my mother Jane looked into my swollen, scrunched up baby face and declared to all assembled, "It's my Granny Willa—come back." She'd written this fateful news on my birth announcements. And, every year on my birthday, she'd tap on her glass with a spoon, stand up, and say, "The moment I looked into Agatha's face, I knew she was my big-hearted, sensible, caretaking, Granny Willa reincarnated."

My mother's insistence about who I had once been had determined the course of my life. I took on the responsibility for other peoples' lives. People depended on me to listen to their woes and to get them out of trouble. And whether it was nature or nurture, I was the one level-headed, introverted female in an extended family of scatter-brained extroverts.

But, beneath whatever Granny Willa qualities I possessed, there lurked a stand-up-for-yourself, say-no, warrior woman. And it was the suppressed Amazon side of me that had risen up to allow me to break my engagement to Jake. Perhaps if I could suppress my self-sacrificing Granny Willa side and embolden my Amazon side, I could change my life. I could let other people fend for themselves as best they could, leaving me with the time and energy to work on things I wanted to work on—like myself.

I looked down the dark road in the direction of the café. No car headlights showed. For the first time in our bumpy relationship, Jake didn't follow me, take me in his arms, and kiss away my anger and hurt.

I got to my feet and moved back into the shadows of the front porch, trying to figure out what to do next. Did I want to stay in this small town and live a life similar to Aunt Bee's in Mayberry—puttering about, taking care of my family, and fixing up food baskets for the needy? Or should I heed the voice that urged me to leave?

I made my choice.

I was leaving.

Tomorrow, I'd be on the early morning train headed for the big city of Millerton. But first, I had to pack and get out of the house before my grandmother or my mother woke up, discovered what I was up to, and talked me out of leaving.

I eased open the front door, stepped inside and, in slow motion, pulled the door closed until I heard the latch make a soft click. I tiptoed toward my room, listening for the sounds of someone stirring. The only noises I heard were the senseless mumblings and light snores of people sleeping—so far, so good.

I dragged my two dust-covered suitcases from under my bed and wiped them off with an old T-shirt. I retrieved my backpack from the closet and started taking things out of my drawers.

Essentials, like my underwear, went into the suitcases. The space in my backpack I reserved for sentimental items like family photos and my pink diary with the tiny lock and key that I'd written in every day during my seventh grade year.

Seventh grade was the year I gave my heart to a sweet boy named Jake who had turned into a louse. I found a tissue and blew my nose. Some of my best years and my most copious tears had been wasted on Jake. But I was moving on. My anguishing over his lack of trustworthiness was at an end.

I sorted through the papers and notebooks in my desk, destroying every For My Eyes Only jotting I came across. I uncapped a pen and filled half a sheet of lined notebook paper with an explanation of what happened tonight and the reason I'd left town.

I tore up the rambling note. No matter what I said in my defense, my family wouldn't understand. Fidelity wasn't always a priority for them. They counted on me to pay the bills on time, keep track of their appointments, and make sure the refrigerator was filled with something more than ice cream and sour milk.

I had no doubt the sordid tale of my behavior was circulating among the late-night crowd and the circulation would pick up speed as soon as Jolly's opened for breakfast. My family would learn the details from eyewitnesses.

So, my new note was short.

"I'm fine. I'll let you know where to find me once I'm settled. Please return the knife to Jolly's. And don't buy meat at the grocery store until the weekly specials are announced."

I folded the paper in half, stuck it in the frame of my mirror and centered the knife on top of the dresser. I zipped all of the zippers on my luggage, checked the drawers and peered into my closet one last time. I turned the knob on my bedroom door.

The toilet flushed.

My heart took off like a racehorse out of the start gate. If it was my grandmother, and she came to check on me as she often did, my goose was cooked. Breathing hard, and thinking fast, I stepped back from the door. If I heard footsteps approaching, I'd hide in my closet. Seeing my bed hadn't been slept in, she'd think I was still out with Jake.

A door shut. I freed the lungful of air I'd been holding captive, and waited ten minutes to give whoever had gotten up enough time to get back to sleep. But I couldn't wait a minute longer if I was going to catch the early train.

I opened my door and scanned the hallway. Both my mother's and my grandmother's bedroom doors were closed.

My nerves pinged from an irrational panic. At thirty-two, I shouldn't need anyone's permission to go anywhere. I should be free to walk away in full daylight giving no explanation of where I was heading or why. But experience had taught me my Granny Willa side would rationalize away the desires of my Amazon.

A plea from my mother or my grandmother to give up such a foolhardy idea, reconcile with Jake, and have the big wedding I'd been planning for years would reverse my decision.

I shouldered my backpack, picked up my suitcases and headed for the front door. For once in my life, my luck held. I got out of the house without being questioned.

I walked the short distance to the train depot. By the time I got to the faded-red, wood-sided building, the sun was peeking over the horizon.

I pulled open one of the depot's heavy, double doors. The interior was deserted except for the station clerk who stood behind the barred window of the ticket counter. He greeted me with a yawn, fingered his stubble and scrutinized me over a pair of eyeglasses perched halfway down his nose.

I stood on the customer side of the counter and

looked through the bars. A half-eaten sausage biscuit sat on his side of the divided counter. My stomach growled. I hadn't taken one bite of the cheeseburger or of anything else I'd ordered at Jolly's last night. Yesterday's lunch, a small salad and a pack of soda crackers, was the last food I'd had. And there wasn't enough time to run across the street and grab something to eat before the train was due.

The clerk took a noisy sip from a cardboard cup.

I eyed the remainder of his sausage biscuit. My mouth watered. After my family, the thing I'd miss most about my hometown was Biscuit City's sausage biscuits. I was tempted to turn around, buy a tall coffee and a biscuit and go home. I could leave tomorrow.

I swallowed the excess saliva pooling in my cheeks. There'd be food and coffee on the train. And freeing myself from everything this town contained—even the good things—was why I was running away.

"Ahem." The station manager tapped his pen on the counter.

"Yes. Sorry. A one-way ticket to Millerton." I pressed my knees against the wall to stop their shaking and watched the clerk prepare my ticket. I handed over my money. He slipped the ticket through the slot, wished me a good trip and stared at me with bloodshot eyes full of questions.

I stared back. Years ago, this man had been married to one of my aunts—her third or fourth in a string of husbands. I had no doubt an early bird had come in to tell him about the commotion at Jolly's last night. And before long another concerned citizen or two would drop by to chat about the excitement. The station clerk would add the details of my departure to the sad tale. I wasn't about to answer his questions so he could add my responses too.

I smiled and nodded, picked up my belongings and headed for the door. As soon as I was out of range of the station clerk's eyes, I dropped my fake smile and slowed my steps. My nerves and my doubts partnered in a dizzying waltz.

Keep going. If you lose your courage, your future is predictable and it isn't pretty.

I started down the platform toward the sign that informed passengers to board here. With each step, the gray-weathered planks groaned. The smell of smoke, from a smoldering woods fire, clung to the breeze. From a tree next to the station, a robin swooped down, landed on a patch of grass, and began hunting for his breakfast. Life had a gentle rhythm here. All news got ground to a fine grit in the gossip mill, but people cared for one another.

I stopped at the designated wait spot, set down my suitcases and placed my backpack atop one of my suitcases.

Had my mother's real Granny Willa been content with her role as a self-sacrificing, forgiving, do-gooder? Or had she dreamed of more? I sensed she'd dreamed of more. But given the times and the lack of opportunity for women, she couldn't find a way out and had made the best of her circumstances.

But times changed. Women had options. Unlike

Granny Willa, I could transform the circumstances and myself. If she was in a position to know, I hoped she was pleased.

Seconds later, the wail of the train whistle split the silence. I slung my backpack over my shoulder and lifted my suitcases so I'd be ready to board as soon as the passenger car door opened and the steps were let down.

The train chugged into the station. I took a last wistful look down the platform.

Yikes.

A female figure had rounded the far corner of the station and was heading my way. My throat clenched. My heart sank. I elbowed the conductor aside, hustled up the steps, and dashed through three cars in a crouch. I plopped down in the aisle seat of an unoccupied row and slumped down, keeping my head lower than the window.

The conductor hollered all aboard. The train started moving. My sigh gushed out like steam when the train's brakes were released.

The train picked up speed. I'd done it. I was on my way to create the new me.

I sat up and looked through the window. My grandmother stood on the platform, the hem of her nightgown showed below the bottom edge of her raincoat. Pink curlers dotted her head. Her hands were cupped around her mouth as if she was shouting. Had the station clerk called the house and told her I was leaving town? Or had she found my note?

I waved.

My eyes watered. The wood smoke in the air had kicked up my allergies. I wiped my cheeks dry and watched my hometown slip from view.

The train tracks ran through the farms on the outskirts of town. The Jamisons' dairy cows were huddled near the entrance of their barn. And then only fields of soybeans were left to see before the train moved out of the county.

Closing my eyes, I breathed deep and let go of the tension in my shoulders.

I opened my eyes. I wanted to keep remembering happy times, but hunger pains were making an audible grumbling in my tummy and interrupting my day-dreaming.

I went in search of the train's snack bar.

I eyed the limited menu and placed my order. The sleepy female attendant filled a cardboard container with coffee and plucked a cellophane-wrapped pimento cheese sandwich from the rack of prepared sandwiches. I paid and dumped two containers of cream into coffee whose color and consistency reminded me of molasses.

Back in my seat, I tore the wrapper off the sandwich, lifted the cut side to my nose and sniffed. The filling smelled okay, but if there'd been anywhere else to buy something to eat and drink I would have tossed the coffee and the sandwich in the trash.

To satisfy the demands of my stomach, I ate the sandwich with its cardboard bread and gummy filling, drank the oily coffee and vowed I'd die of hunger before I'd buy another thing to eat from the train's snack bar.

The day brightened as the sun rose higher. I knew no one in Millerton. I'd visited twice—once in my teens and a second time in my twenties. I was familiar with the layout of the commercial and tourist areas. But this time I wouldn't be visiting—I would be making Millerton my home. I'd need to become familiar with the different residential areas and find a cheap place to rent in a safe and convenient part of town.

My Granny Willa side kicked in creating doubts about making such a rash move. And, to add to my other misgivings, she tossed in a sobering fact.

Getting out of your box and dumping the people who love you out of your life means you have only yourself to blame when you lose your nerve and settle for less than you want.

My hand shook as I searched through my backpack for the tissues I'd tucked in at the last minute. To minimize the effect of her warning, I filled my mind with the words of my favorite childhood story—I think I can, I think I can.

By the time the train pulled into Millerton station, three hundred and twenty-two miles southeast of my hometown, I'd damped down all qualms, folded up my habit of backing down when challenged, and stored all dispiriting thoughts in an imaginary lockbox.

I stepped off the train and took deep breaths of air free of wood smoke. The conductor had recommended a respectable hotel within walking distance. I set off following his directions.

A sense of being unbound lifted my spirit. I no longer

had anyone to please but myself. I no longer had to fill the role of caretaker for people whose lives were full of chaos. Or fit into my mother's preconceived notion of who I was. In Millerton, the real me could bloom.

Farewell, Granny Willa.

Chapter Two

Within a week of arriving in Millerton, I'd found two part–time jobs that paid enough for me to survive if I wasn't extravagant. And I'd leased a low-rent former building superintendent's furnished basement apartment in a luxury building.

The walls of my apartment were painted institution green, the furnishings were worn. The windows were typical basement windows, small and high up in the wall. But, in case of fire, I was told they could be opened wide enough for a person to get through.

The building fronted on a street serviced by the city bus line. A doorman was on duty from six in the morning until midnight. An attendant was behind the counter in the lobby every day from nine until five. Despite the flaws of my apartment, it was a lucky find. And for the first time in my life, I had a place of my own.

My introvert nature delighted in the solitary and

quiet space. My nerves calmed. I no longer had to expect sudden bursts of noise and motion riling my nerves. Each time I stepped inside my apartment and closed the door behind me, I embraced the silence and breathed a big sigh of relief.

Two weeks after I'd moved in, I'd sent my family my address and phone number. Christy, my sister, had called twice to fill me in on the ongoing drama that was her life. My mother, the actress and seer, had sent me a dozen red roses with a card congratulating me on my performance in Jolly's Café. But, my grandmother was maintaining an unnerving and unnatural silence.

My days were full. I'd checked out and read every self-help book in the library. I'd watched numerous stop-messing-up-your-life shows on television. When I wasn't working at my paying jobs, I was working on a detailed plan to bench my Granny Willa persona and get my inner Amazon onto the field.

On the day designated to put my plan into action, I woke before the alarm clock went off. My stomach started to rumble like a rockslide. What had I been thinking? A disturbance in the natural order of things could lead to a disaster. I considered postponing my re-birthday until the next auspicious day. But, the shriek of my trusty alarm clock put an end to my thoughts of turning over and going back to sleep.

I thrust out my hand to end the raucous noise. The slight disturbance in the air flow resulted in big trouble. Instead of locating the alarm button, my hand whacked the side of the clock, toppling it off the nightstand. The sound of my faithful wind-up clock, with the two silver bells on top that made it resemble Mr. Potato Head with a set of ears attached, crashing into silence on a linoleum-tile floor should have set off warning bells. But I refused to give significant meaning to the demise of my clock. Accidents happened, and for no reason.

Sharp contractions rippled my midsection, forcing me into a sitting position. Was Granny Willa creating internal pain in an attempt to sabotage my attempt to demote her to the second team?

Then I remembered the box of chocolates I'd eaten last night to remove the temptation which could cause me to break my vow of healthy eating in the days ahead.

Get up, a voice in my head said. *Get out of bed. Start your engines*. The words were faint, but my inner Amazon was trying to get through to me. I hastened to obey before she gave up.

Throwing off the bedcovers, I covered a yawn and folded myself into a semblance of the lotus position. I began to clear my mind.

My spirits soared. My plan to depose Granny Willa and empower my inner Amazon was underway.

Breathing measured breaths, I spoke aloud my new life motto.

"From this day forward, my needs, my desires, my goals and my happiness come first."

Selfish! My nag, who showed up at inconvenient moments, scolded. *About time*, my Amazon voice shouted.

I steeled myself to having a continuous battle of words between my nag, my Granny Willa, and my inner Amazon until one of them emerged victorious.

I hummed "The Star Spangled Banner" to drown out the nag. I hit each note of the national anthem's melody on key until I got to the glare note. Hitting the glare note, without thinking or pausing, was something I'd been trying to do since I'd first learned the song. And every attempt had failed.

I stopped humming and recited aloud the pledge I'd written in my new journal. "Each day I, Agatha Marple, will exercise, eat healthy, and maintain absolute control over who and what I allow in my life."

Power surged through me as my words spun like teacups at Disney World and whirled away to ride the world's air currents. With my resolve strengthened and my doubts tamped down, I was well on my way to severing the umbilical cord connecting me to my old self. I slammed the lid on my imaginary lockbox stuffed full of old fears and doubts and took a cleansing breath.

Granny Willa, rest in peace.

The scent of the lavender and thyme candle I'd burned last night still perfumed the basement air. Feeling full of new energy, I leaped out of bed. I brushed my teeth, washed my face and pulled my hair into a ponytail. Dressed in a pair of black running shorts, and a flamingo-pink knit sleeveless shirt, I tugged a rainbow-striped sweatband around my head. I slid my feet into my new running shoes designed like tanks for the combat jogger.

Ready, set, go.

In the front room—the combined living, dining and kitchen area of my two-room apartment—I stuck a gold star on the chart I'd created and secured to my refrigerator with magnets. The glittery star sparkled in the first square of the column titled EXERCISE. I hadn't earned this star yet, but seeing it there boosted my morale.

And then my disloyal eyes eyed the coffeemaker on the kitchen counter. Every nerve in my body thrummed with a desire for their morning jolt of caffeine.

I dashed out the front door of my apartment, rode the service elevator to the first floor lobby and hustled out of the building.

On the sidewalk, I sucked in enough oxygen mixed with exhaust fumes to fill my lungs and headed for the corner of McKenna and South a half block away.

My waffle-soled jogging shoes slapped the cement sidewalk. I picked up speed. The sun heated the moisture-laden air. In another hour or two, the outdoors would be a hot-air bath. Reality replaced jubilation. The backs of my expensive new jogging shoes rode up and down my heels like department store elevators moving between floors on sale days.

Trying to ignore the irritation, I bit the inside of my bottom lip to create a second source of pain. I began humming the theme of *Star Wars* and imaged the gold star on my chart to keep myself from stopping, taking off the ill-fitting shoes, and tossing them into a city trash bin.

I crossed South Street, whizzed by the dry cleaners, the pharmacy, and the used bookstore. Halfway to the next corner, I gasped for air. The sound of blood pulsing in my ears blocked out all other sounds.

I slowed my pace.

And then I got a break. The flashing red hand of the pedestrian signal forced me to stop. I stepped in place while waiting to cross. My ragged breathing evened out.

One should begin a new exercise program gradually to build up one's endurance.

Those exact words, lisped into the television airwaves by a bald-headed guy with a squeaky voice and lumpy arms bounced into my thoughts—words I'd heard but failed to heed.

The safe-to-cross icon blinked. The icon displayed the perfect walking technique—an even stride, arms pumping.

Crossing Main at a fast walk, my arms and legs moving in a synchronized pattern, I was re-energized. I was on the right track now thanks to the safe-to-cross icon and the words of a lisping, infomercial guy. My lungs functioned properly, my ears picked up traffic sounds. Ignoring the voice of my nag who'd said something about toxic air particles causing cancer, I filled my lungs with polluted city air.

And then—in the middle of the third block—the smell of donuts frying forced me to a standstill. My nose twitched. My mouth watered. My lips opened and closed like a fish. But it wasn't oxygen I craved—it was the energizing boost supplied by caffeine and sugar. And the door of Koenig's Bake Shop was the flimsy barrier between me and the means of satisfying my addiction.

I bit down hard on my lower lip, uttered a whimper, and forced my feet past the bakeshop door, past the picture window with its red-checked curtain skirt and

KOENIG'S BAKE SHOP written across it in an arc of black script. I got as far as the connecting seam of the adjoining building before turning back.

I turned the knob and pushed open the bakeshop door.

Standing behind the sale counter, Gerda Koenig's plump face beamed a proprietor's welcome. And then her expression turned sour. Her lips turned down. Tsk-tsk sounds telegraphed a rebuke.

Granny Willa stirred in the pit of my stomach—the *me* who couldn't disappoint others took charge.

"Why you run past my bakeshop today?" Gerda asked.

The sharp tone in her voice was the exact tone my nag used to activate my guilt button. My nag added a second jab—*you made Gerda unhappy*.

"We got plenty fresh donuts today, Chicky."

Of course they had fresh donuts. Donuts were their specialty. And every inch of me wanted to sit down and eat one of those donuts like I had every morning since I'd moved here.

My right hand clutched my tummy. Muscle twitches zipped back and forth between my shoulder blades. Granny Willa surged into my throat, forming a big lump. The shuffling of my feet kept time with Gerda's finger wagging.

"I didn't plan to stop today," I squeaked. My Amazon side struggled to rise to my rescue. I sounded pitiful. And then my Amazon voice pierced through the clatter going on inside my head. *Where is it written one must consume fattening food to please others?*

I squared my shoulders. "Ahem." Lowering my voice an octave and enunciating each word, I tried to explain to Gerda why I'd run past. "I've begun exercising and eating a healthy diet, Gerda. It's a . . ."

Gerda's chest inflated like a hot air balloon. Her lack of a waistline evidenced her disdain for healthy eating.

"Why Chicky? Every morning I wait to see your pretty face come in my door. I see your happy smile, I'm happy. And now you say crazy things, I'm sad."

". . . new plan for . . ." My words trailed off as my Granny Willa side rolled over my immature defense against other peoples' stated and unstated needs.

I stepped across the threshold but kept my shoulder against the door to prevent it from closing all the way—a desperate move to preserve my chance of earning my gold star today for healthy eating.

And then I made a fatal error—I inhaled.

The spicy, sugary air destroyed my effort to triumph over temptation.

Simple Simon met a pie man . . .

My shoulders slumped forward. The click of the door latch sounded a death knell for my healthy eating star.

I took a step toward the sale counter. A cup of coffee would satisfy my need for caffeine. And stirring half a packet of sugar into Gerda's strong coffee would satisfy my sweet tooth.

Do not order a donut.

Tomorrow, I would give up artificial stimulants—again.

"A cup of coffee," I said taking two more halting steps toward the counter. "I've made a new plan for my life, Gerda. Healthy food, daily exercise, meditation, and positive thoughts."

In a burst of bravado, I covered the remaining distance to prove to Gerda it wasn't her or her business I was rejecting. "I—"

Gerda pulled her ample chest up and dropped her chin. Her upper body formed a solid block. Her eyes narrowed. Her fists sunk into the flesh of her hips.

"Koenig's pastries are healthy. Never do we use nothing spoiled. Never do we get a ninety-eight score from the health department inspectors. Ninety-nine and Ninety-nine dot five is what we get." Her indignation singed the ends of her words. At any moment flames would shoot from her mouth.

I averted my gaze from her face to the thirty varieties of glazed, frosted, powdered and plain donuts perched in the glass–fronted case. Their tempting plumpness proved too powerful to resist at this early stage of my transformation.

Tomorrow, I would retake the pledge to avoid eating food that wasn't good for me.

"A chocolate frosted with mixed nut topping," I said.

Gerda grinned and softened the set of her shoulders. She resembled the warm, motherly person I knew her as.

"Sit down, Chicky." Her smile was a winner's smile. "I'll serve you." Her dimpled fingers reached across the glass counter and patted my hand.

I turned around to survey the small eat-in area. Two of the five red-mottled Formica-topped tables were occupied. At each of those tables, a man sat forward in a chair with his knees splayed and his bulging stomach hanging over his belt. A coffee cup and an empty plate sat atop both tables.

Rats.

A three-way duel between my warring sides started inside my head. The commotion blocked the positive thoughts needed to counter my negative thoughts. My plan was spiraling downward. My willpower was weak. At the first provocation, I had fallen into my old patterns. Perhaps I was trying to change too much too fast.

I sat down.

The man at the table nearest to the door got up, threw some change on the table then waddled out.

My sweatband felt clammy. My temples throbbed. Blisters would be forming on my heels where the skin had been rubbed off. My bare legs stuck to the vinyl chair seat. Misery filled every inch of my being. My re-birthday day, a day that should have been a day of joy, had turned into a day of despair.

I slumped in the tipsy, metal-legged chair, and stared out the window watching people pass the bakeshop without twitching their nose or glancing inside. It was clear that I'd been born with an ultra-sensitive olfactory nerve. Maybe in another life, maybe even centuries before Granny Willa showed up, I'd been a truffle pig or a bloodhound or a perfume tester—a creature whose job required a keen sense of smell.

But, in my present state, my sensory gift led me to ruin.

Chapter Three

Maybe I should stop fighting fate. I was Granny Willa reincarnated and no amount of effort on my part would change this. I would sublet my apartment and move back to the neon-green house with the pink shutters, sit on the porch after supper, and enter my pickles in the Newcombe County Fair every year. I glanced at the donut display case. Did my mother's Granny Willa have a weakness for donuts too?

All of the self-help books made one thing clear; when the going gets tough, losers abandon their goal. I hardened my resolve.

I squared my shoulders and aligned the discs of my spine. Good posture is the key to clear thinking, my second-grade teacher said every morning when we lined up for recess.

"Tsk, tsk, tsk." Gerda's chastising sounds interrupted

my effort to summon help from my inner Amazon to refuse the donut.

A coffee mug was in one of Gerda's hands and the plate with my donut was in the other.

I inhaled the coffee's enticing aroma and eyed the donut's chocolate icing glistening beneath a generous sprinkling of nuts.

Gerda shifted the donut plate to the same hand as the coffee mug and then began moving the index finger of her free hand back and forth like a windshield wiper whisks away rain.

"You find a smile to put on your face, Chicky. Today is a good day."

Looking happy wasn't my goal—being happy was. And succeeding at being happy was harder than I'd expected.

As soon as I appeased my sinful cravings, I'd buy a clock radio to replace my broken alarm clock. And then I'd return to my apartment, get back into bed and wrap myself in a cocoon of my green fuzzy blanket until it was time to get ready for my shift at Mitzi's Diner.

Tomorrow, awakened by soothing music instead of a shrill ring, I'd renew my efforts to change my unhealthy lifestyle.

The man seated at the second table laughed, looked up from the newspaper he'd been reading, crossed his eyes and waggled his eyebrows at me. Caught off-guard, my perfidious lips turned upward without permission.

He nodded and smiled back.

Gerda stopped wagging her finger. "That's better, Chicky." She rewarded my smile by setting the donut plate and the coffee mug on the table. "You're a beautiful woman, Chicky. Enjoy life. Don't be sad."

The shower of encouraging words caused me to sniff and look down at the table. "Thanks, Gerda. I'm trying." I couldn't explain to her why I was sad. She wouldn't understand why failing the test of her bakeshop upset me.

"And don't worry, Chicky. Worry carves lines on the face."

I looked up and smiled.

"Good. You look better now," she said. "Younger."

I clung to her words like a drowning person clings to an overturned boat. Improving my appearance with a smile cost nothing.

Gerda cleared the used dishes from the first table and headed back to the counter.

I circled the ceramic coffee mug with my hands and stared into the brown depths that revealed nothing.

The sound of a chair scooting across the floor made me look up. The remaining male customer had pushed away from his table and risen to his feet. He gave me a thumbs up and waved to Gerda. She called good-bye to him as he went out and then disappeared to the kitchen.

I was alone in the public area.

I licked my lips and concentrated my eyes for a moment on the beauty of Mr. Koenig's donut artistry. I removed the plastic utensils from their paper napkin case and plunged the serrated knife into the heart of the baker's art and sawed the donut into halves.

Picking up one half of the grease-and-sugar-laden donut, I took my first bite. The primitive satisfaction from indulging my unnatural lust for donuts compensated me for my worries about healthy eating. How could anything this delicious be unhealthy?

I ran my tongue around my lips to recover any specks of frosting left behind, released my thighs from the suction of the chair seat, and retrieved an abandoned newspaper from the table in front of me. I found the classified section and folded it over to the job listings.

Currently, I took assignments from a temp agency during the day, waited tables at Mitzi's Diner four nights a week and kept up my search for my dream job—a job that promised me adventure, would make use of my degree in art history, and offered good pay and benefits. I ran my finger down the column of today's listings—pizza delivery, window washer, car detailer—nothing worth pursuing. I turned to the car ads and studied the prices of used cars while I ate and drank.

I came to the end of the FOR SALE BY OWNER column and glanced down at my plate. Only crumbs and droppings remained. Somehow, I'd eaten both halves of the donut without being aware of what I was doing.

Drats.

I looked around. Gerda hadn't returned. I eyed the surface of the plate dotted with nuts, frosting and crumbs. Running my finger around the dish, I mopped up the stray bits. And then, to savor every last morsel of my last—I promise—Koenig's donut, I stuck my finger into my mouth.

I began reading the review of a new restaurant in Millerton as I sucked the nuts and frosting and crumbs off. I had started the slow withdrawal of my finger when the air in the bakeshop changed. Ominous prickles tiptoed along the nape of my neck and danced at my hairline. I glanced up from the newspaper.

A man, dressed in a navy-blue suit, a white shirt and a red tie stood behind Koenig's sale counter. His eagle-like eyes focused on me as if I were a rabbit he was considering for dinner. I yanked my finger out of my mouth and turned my head toward the window to hide the rush of heat flooding into my face. Picking up the coffee mug, I drained the contents—forgetting Gerda's coffee came with the grounds. Gritty particles filled my mouth. I rolled my tongue around my teeth to remove as many as I could and then wiped off my tongue with my napkin. I swallowed. Grounds scraped down my throat.

Get a grip. Dressed in the colors of the American flag, the prissy, eagle-eyed man was likely a road-weary salesman hoping to land a big order for his company's multi-hued candy sprinkles.

I rearranged the newspaper on the table and pretended to read. From my protective posture, I rotated my eyes until I could see the sale counter and the man.

My Amazon, my nag and my Granny Willa were quiet. But my survival instincts urged me to rush out of this bakeshop—this den of misfortune—before I found myself in another kind of battle.

Like Hansel and Gretel, my sweet tooth had lured me into this trap. But I couldn't leave. The eagle-eyed man was behind the counter—and my thighs were exposed.

Gerda came through the door from the kitchen. The man turned his back to the public area, leaned against the edge of the counter and appeared to be talking to her.

If I hurried, I could get out of here without further scrutiny.

I slid my chair back. The metal legs scraped across the tiles with a spine-tingling screech. I sprang to my feet. My right hip struck the corner edge of the table.

"Umph." My reaction to the pain sounded loud. But neither Gerda nor the eagle-eyed man turned to look at me.

My line of sight zeroed in on the front door. Taking long strides, I headed for the exit.

"Chicky. Stop." Gerda's command startled me into stopping—the second fatal error of the day.

"Come and meet my Dirky," she said, puffing out her chest and her cheeks.

So the raptor-eyed man, whose outfit would be perfect for the Fourth of July, wasn't a salesman. He was Gerda's son, Dirky. And according to Gerda's previous descriptions of her Dirky, he never got less than ninety-nine dot nine—on anything.

My upper and lower teeth fused. A warning growl rumbled in the pit of my queasy stomach. My escape was four or five giant steps away. My feet were stuffed into a pair of expensive running shoes.

I pivoted.

In the wrong direction.

And took five giant steps forward. I offered my hand to Dirky.

"Agatha Marple," I said keeping my lips tight to conceal any nuts or coffee grounds stuck in my teeth.

I was out of control.

His right eyebrow shot up. Amusement sparked in his

eyes. Getting a reaction when I gave my name was no surprise. I no longer blurted out how my mother, Jane, loved mystery novels and how she'd married my father for the sole purpose of acquiring the Marple name for herself and her future children. And then, after naming me Agatha and my sister Christy, had filed for divorce.

"Dirk Koenig," he said as he shook my hand. His brown–flecked topaz eyes, framed by long dark lashes, scrutinized my face. I managed not to blink. His handshake was firm. I tightened my grip. His smile exposed a set of pearled teeth. I broadened my closed-lip smile.

He leaned toward me. Confident. Sure of himself. Secure in the effect he had on women—the effect he knew he was having on me. These were the conceits common to men raised by doting, noncritical mothers—self-absorbed men—the kind of men smart women avoided.

My wind died. My sails collapsed. I couldn't move.

Gerda watched us with a mischievous glow in her eyes.

"Agatha comes to our bakeshop each day since she moved here. She has perfect attendance."

I was on track for earning a Koenig's Bake Shop perfect attendance certificate like the one I'd earned from Sunday School when I was ten.

"Welcome to Millerton and to Koenig's bakery, Miss Marple." His gaze skipped over my body. He pursed his lips.

I longed to cover my exposed thighs with my hands, but I sensed a protective action would confirm my lack of confidence and afford this man a win I didn't want him to have.

"Thanks."

Dirk's gaze drifted back to my face. "I hope you'll continue to visit Koenig's." He lips flickered into a smile.

And then he turned to face his mother.

I stared at the back of his head.

He spoke to Gerda in a low tone of voice.

I'd been dismissed. And my inner Amazon was nowhere to be found.

I started for the door of Koenig's—unhappy—bakeshop.

"Bye, Chicky," Gerda called. "See you tomorrow."

I waved and then vowed I'd never step foot in Koenig's Bake Shop again. And, until my defenses were strengthened, I'd avoid going anywhere near their bakeshop. Furthermore, if I had the misfortune of encountering her Dirky again, a man who could turn out to be as tempting as their donuts, I'd make clear to him the contempt I harbored for spoiled, pampered men.

Once I was outside, my Amazon emerged from hiding. I perked up and turned in the direction of my apartment building. Granny Willa clawed her way back onto center stage. At the cross street, despite my yearning not to get emotional over every little setback, tears filled my eyes. Not only had I given into my love of donuts, but when introduced to Dirk I had wilted.

As I waited for the light to change, I knew I was at a literal and virtual crossroad.

"Granny Willa, say something."

Wimp.

I laughed out loud. "Thanks," I muttered.

I spoke positive words out loud to double their impact.

"Courage. You're a beautiful woman. Gerda said so.

You're kind. You're worthy of respect. Stand up straight. Look happy. Be confident." My uplifting words changed my mood. I would not be defeated by a stranger's rude behavior.

"Hello," I said in a cheery voice to the neighborhood homeless guy pushing a grocery cart with his possessions along the sidewalk.

He rolled his eyes and made an unpleasant sound.

I responded to his derisive salute with, "Have a nice day." A cheerful attitude creates a cache of goodwill. Mumbling to himself, he rolled on past me.

The crossing signal blinked. The walking figure icon replaced the red hand. Crossing signal icons never quit, and neither would I. With every setback, every attempt to break my spirit, I'd fight back harder.

But first, as soon as I got to my apartment, I'd go over the astrological chart calculations I'd made to determine an auspicious day for my re-birthday and find the error. And then I'd recalculate and find a right day to begin my transformation.

Chapter Four

I entered my apartment. A red number one was blinking on my answering machine. I sighed, tossed my keys on the table, and pushed the play button.

I toed off a running shoe.

My sister's voice boomed through the speaker. "Agatha, if you're not sitting, sit. When you hear what I'm going to tell you, I'm pretty sure you'll faint."

My sister thrived on creating chaos in her life and in other peoples' lives. I ignored her warning.

A long pause ensued. But I could hear breathing.

I pulled off the damp sweatband, opened the freezer door, and filled a glass with ice cubes.

Her lengthy pause was meant to heighten my anxiety. I filled the glass with water.

Christy gave a strangled sound. "Okay. Sitting or not, here goes." She added a sigh before continuing. "I bumped into Mr. Dent yesterday afternoon." Her voice

36

lowered to a conspiratorial whisper. "In Biglow's produce section. Next to the melon display."

I paid closer attention to what she was saying. Mr. Dent was Momma Dolly's beau.

"My shopping cart nudged his hip. It startled him. The cantaloupe he'd been sniffing hit the floor and splattered. It made a terrible mess. The produce clerk couldn't have been nicer but . . ."

My sister was being charged with reckless driving of a grocery cart. My right hand covered my heart.

". . . anyway, I would've called you yesterday to tell you this, but I was in a rush to get to the drug store in Cranston to pick up Jed's nasal spray so I could get to the meeting of the historical society on time and then in the middle of the meeting Clifford's play school called. He'd thrown up on his teacher. I had to pick him up early, and then I had to get supper started—beef stew takes a while—and then I forgot. This morning I remembered. Are you sitting, Ags?"

My protective instinct urged me to sit. I didn't. I couldn't believe whatever she had to tell me was so terrible I'd faint. I stayed on my feet, but gripped the back of a chair, just in case.

"After Mr. Dent removed a big chunk of melon from his shoe, he told me Momma Dolly left town and was headed for Millerton."

My sister spoke with a clear enunciation of each syllable. There was no misunderstanding of what she'd said. Momma Dolly, our energetic, flamboyant grandmother, was on her way to Millerton to invade my coveted, solitary world.

I was going to die. For once my sister underestimated the impact of what she had to say. The sharp pains in my chest were the beginning of a fatal heart attack.

It was foolish of me to save money by doing the calculations for my astrological chart on my own. If I'd paid an expert to do my chart, the news of an unexpected visitor wouldn't have come as such a shock. I collapsed on my couch to avoid the embarrassment of being found lying in a heap on the cold green tiles of my apartment floor, and waited for the end.

Don't get me wrong, I love Momma Dolly, my maternal grandmother. For years, she took care of Christy and me while our mother worked as a bit-part actress. But Momma Dolly is an imaginative dreamer with a dynamic personality. An hour spent with her is exhausting. When she got here, she'd take over, and I'd be caught up in the whirlpool of anxiety she stirs in my introvert's soul. All of my energy would be used up dealing with her. My work on moving my inner Amazon into the dominant position would suffer a setback more serious than the setback caused by miscalculating the favorable day to begin shedding my self-defeating habits.

I got up and stabbed the delete button on the answering machine, as if by deleting my sister's message I could reverse Momma Dolly's direction. I began wringing my hands together and pacing around the center of my front room. But all of my fretful activity was useless. Nothing I did would stop Momma Dolly from showing up at my door. My only escape was to pack up and run away again—leaving no forwarding address and then never contacting any member of my family to tell them where I'd gone.

I decided to put my escalating anxiety to good use by cleaning up myself and my apartment while I waited for her. I took the chart with the one shiny star off my refrigerator and hid it beneath my underwear in my dresser. I stripped naked, tossed my exercise clothes into the hamper and stepped into my claustrophobic shower.

Lukewarm water leaked around the rim of the showerhead in an erratic course that changed direction on a whim. Tears trickled down my cheeks in the same erratic way. The freedom to pursue my own path had been an illusion—a cruel tease. Not even the witness protection program could deter my grandmother if she wanted to visit me.

Sniffing back my feeling-sorry-for-myself tears, I dressed in clean shorts and a pale blue T-shirt, swept up the pieces of my broken clock and tidied the kitchen area. I mopped the linoleum floors and plumped up the pillows on my secondhand couch. With everything as neat and clean as possible, I clicked on my thirteen-inch television—a bargain buy from a pawn shop. And then I wriggled myself into my one big purchase, a new neon-yellow beanbag chair. I focused my eyes on the images across the tiny screen and my ears on the words coming through the speakers. No child's poem or difficult song in my repertoire was powerful enough to calm my nervous tension. I was counting on the make-believe world of television to blot out my apprehension that was bordering on terror.

The world turned. Someone had children to worry

about. The afternoon soaps rolled on. I switched to a sitcom rerun channel. Three hours later, the theme song for "The Andy Griffith Show" was playing again when the "bzzzzt" of my intercom brought me back from television land. I unwound my legs, got to my feet and dragged myself to the front wall and pushed the button that activated the intercom.

"Yes?"

"A Miss Dolly McWater is here to see you."

Reality slammed into my stomach, leaving me short of breath. Momma Dolly had arrived. I covered a groan with a cough.

"Dolly McWater? Here? What a nice surprise," I croaked. "Send her down at once."

The trip to my apartment from the service elevator wasn't far, but one had to pass gurgling iron pipes, glowing furnaces and valves the size of car tires to get to my door. It was an intimidating passage for the weak and fearful. Momma Dolly was neither weak nor fearful, but she loved having concern shown toward her as if she was. And I couldn't disappoint her.

I headed into the murky, cavernous space of the basement. By the time I reached the elevator, the cage had completed its short descent. The doors slid apart. Framed in the opening was Momma Dolly in all her glory. Curly, bright orange hair, iridescent sky-blue eyelids, lips slathered with fire engine-red lipstick made her as colorful as an Australian King Parrot.

Her full lips formed a wicked grin. Each of her slender hands gripped the leather handles of a large suitcase. On the floor of the elevator was a cardboard box big enough to contain a small air-conditioner.

She stood motionless.

My nose twitched. I sneezed. As soon as I could, I'd buy a supply of allergy pills and a giant-sized bottle of headache pills. But before I could do anything else, I had to extract Momma Dolly from the elevator.

"Am I welcome?" she asked.

"How did you know I missed you?"

I clamped a hand over my traitorous lips. I wanted my self–incriminating words back. But the giant lump in my throat prevented me from retracting my tattletale remark.

A quirk of her eyebrows let me know she was pleased.

"Momma Dolly knows things," she said as her wicked grin widened and her eyes sparkled with delight. "As soon as you stand aside, Agatha, so I can get out of this disgusting elevator, we'll get right to work fixing things."

I could feel the thin rod of my spine melting in the heat of Momma Dolly's supercharged personality.

"Let me take your suitcases," I said holding out my hands.

"Take the box instead." She pointed the toe of one of her bright pink shoes-decorated with multicolored faux jewels—at the large box. "And be careful."

Bending down, I could see holes punched through the cardboard top.

Breathing holes.

I surrounded the sides of the box with my arms and

hefted it upwards, balancing the weight against my chest. A loud yowl sounded. An unhappy creature was inside the makeshift carrier. I glared at Momma Dolly.

"Miss Priss may be upset," Momma Dolly said.

"Who's Miss Priss?"

"Herman Dent's cat."

"Herman let you bring his cat?"

"Not exactly. Herman ignored my pleas to keep Miss Priss in the house so she couldn't stalk and kill innocent birds"—Momma Dolly's voice trembled—"leaving me no recourse but to kidnap her."

The triumphant look in Momma Dolly's eyes silenced my expression of disbelief.

She nodded toward the box. "Miss Priss will no longer reduce the bird population in Herman's neighborhood."

"So, you show up here with stolen goods and put me in jeopardy of being arrested for aiding and abetting a criminal."

I juggled the box to get a better hold.

Momma Dolly stopped walking and swung out a suitcase. My knee bumped into the hard surface.

She turned her head to glare at me.

And then she laughed. And the sound of her hearty and infectious laughter seemed to make the world right again. For a brief moment, I didn't care about her intrusion into my new world nor worry about the chaos that would ensue.

"Yes," she said in between laughs, "I'm on the run from the obstinate and inhumane Herman Dent. But don't worry about being arrested, Agatha. Herman won't call the police. I left a note to tell him I was leaving him and then stuck a post-it note to the cat door to tell him Miss Priss would not be coming home."

I could only hope Herman could see the post-it note. People with perfect eyesight had trouble deciphering Momma Dolly's handwriting and Mr. Dent depended on trifocals to see anything.

But I didn't believe the real reason Momma Dolly stole Herman's cat and drove to Millerton had anything to do with the welfare of birds.

"I'll fix tea and then you can tell me why you ran away from Mr. Dent."

Momma Dolly swung around to look at me. Her shoulder clipped a protruding pipe.

"Interesting place for an apartment," she said.

"I'm happy down here. There are no nosey and noisy neighbors to bother me."

"Which reminds me"—Momma Dolly set her suitcases down and flexed her fingers—"a handsome gentleman wearing a striking blue uniform was standing outside the building's entrance. He helped me with Miss Priss' box and my suitcases—a polite young man, clean shaven and scented with musk. He wasn't wearing a wedding ring. I hope you're considering him as a good prospect Agatha."

"Harold? The doorman?"

"He didn't give his name."

"Harold is in his teens. And—"

"A man in a uniform is fetching, regardless of age."

"Fine, but Harold isn't a man."

"You're kidding, Agatha. I swear there was the shadow of a beard on . . . um . . . the uniformed person's jaw."

"I didn't mean Harold *isn't* a man, only that he's a boy."

Momma Dolly let out her breath. "He isn't a boy, Agatha. He's a young man—a nice looking and a polite young man—with a steady job."

My stomach lurched like a ship on a choppy sea. A Koenig's donut and a cup of coffee weren't sufficient ballast to keep my emotions on an even keel.

"Leave your suitcases here. I'll come back for them," I said to avoid further discussion of Harold's attributes.

Momma Dolly shook her head, grabbed hold of the suitcase handles and, with a look of grim determination, forged on ahead of me.

"The door's ajar. Give it a push," I said.

She pushed the door open with her foot and paused on the threshold. "Women live years longer than men, Agatha. I've buried three myself. According to life insurance statistics, a wise woman chooses to marry a man five to ten years younger. That should put Harold within range."

I nudged my grandmother with Miss Priss' box to spur her to move through the doorway. I wanted to set down the box containing Mr. Dent's killer cat and end this conversation.

Momma Dolly entered my apartment, set her suitcases next to the wall and reached up to re-pin her hair.

"I'll get water heating for tea," I said as I squatted down to rid myself of Miss Priss' box without giving Herman's cat a jarring surprise. "Shall I let Miss Priss out?"

"Leave her in the box for now. Let her settle down. I'm sure she'll welcome some quiet time to recover from being tossed about all day. If I hadn't been in such a hurry to get out of town before Herman learned I'd stolen his cat, I would have stopped by Stimson's Hardware and bought a proper cat carrier."

I longed for an empty box to climb into and recover from a long day of having my emotions tossed about. This apartment had been my box, a place I could recover in, but the arrival of Momma Dolly changed everything.

I took the teakettle from the back burner of the stove and flipped up the lid. I'd call Mitzi at the diner and ask if she could get along without me tonight. If I could get Momma Dolly to reveal the truth about why she'd run away from Herman, it'd be worth the loss of tonight's tips. And if I was lucky, I could convince her to call him, patch up their disagreement, and leave for home in the morning.

I raised my voice to cover the sound of the water splashing into the kettle. "I'll try to get off work tonight."

"No need to miss work, Agatha."

"Are you sure?"

Momma Dolly placed her hands on her hips and gave me her you-can't-be-serious look. "Tell me one time, Agatha, when I said something I didn't mean?"

There was no use arguing. Momma Dolly could be stubborn, and I'd end up going to work anyway. I picked up her suitcases, surprised by how heavy they were, and put them in the bedroom. I hung an extra set of towels in the bathroom and got into my work clothes.

When I emerged, Momma Dolly was sitting on the edge of my sagging sofa, holding the TV clicker in one hand and a mug with a teabag tab hanging over the side in her other.

"It's time for my story, Agatha. I'm worried to death about Jade."

Momma Dolly had been worrying about Jade, a character on her favorite soap opera, for as long as I could remember. I took a box of cheese crackers from the cupboard, ate a handful and poured some into a bowl which I set on the table.

Momma Dolly leaned closer to the television. "Jade always falls for a wrong man and then suffers serious consequences from having made a bad choice. But this time, she's not only fallen for a wrong man, I'm pretty sure her new wrong man is a killer." Momma Dolly narrowed her eyes and peered at the television. "Look Agatha. There he is. The tall man on the right. Look at his eyes."

I squinted to get a better look at Jade's newest wrong man's eyes. "He looks fine."

"He does not look fine, Agatha. Something is not right about him. Sometimes, when he lights a cigarette, his hand shakes. Once, he glared at Jade from across the room in a sinister manner. It was frightening. I'm thinking about phoning the director to warn him about this man. If Jade is killed, half of the audience will turn off the show forever."

"Then you should call. For starters, her newest wrong man smokes cigarettes and the secondhand smoke could kill her." I paused for several seconds, and Momma Dolly ignored me. "Crime statistics show that ninety-nine percent of serial killers are chain-smokers," I added because I felt peevish and disoriented over her invasion of my sanctuary.

Momma Dolly didn't react. When she watched her story, she blocked out everything else.

"I need to go," I said with a sense of relief at leaving Jade to her fictional misfortunes. "There are cans of soup in the cupboard and a box of soda crackers on top of the refrigerator."

Momma Dolly sighed. "Hmm." Her eyes didn't move from the screen. I grabbed my backpack, slung it over my shoulder, and hurried out the apartment door.

Hey diddle, diddle, the cat and the fiddle . . .

I stood at the curb near the shelter waiting for the city bus. I checked my watch. I was early. The bus wouldn't be along for another ten minutes or so. Shifting my stance, I let the strap of my backpack slide down my arm, shielded my eyes against the sun and looked in the direction the bus would come from.

A sleek, low-slung sports car, polished to a high gleam, eased to the curb in front of me and stopped. The passenger side window slid down in one smooth, noise-less motion. Thinking someone wanted to ask directions, I bent over to speak to them.

Dirk Koenig's eagle eyes stared at me. In the car's dim interior, his silky golden hair shone.

"Hi." His voice sounded warm and friendly.

My inner Amazon tried to surface.

Dirk smiled.

She fell back.

My inner Amazon had weaknesses too.

The disdain I'd sworn to show Dirk if I encountered him again was unavailable—shunted to the side by his nice-guy act.

Rats.

"We met in my parents' bakeshop . . ."

The wrestling match inside my head, between my nag who urged me to straighten up and ignore him, my Amazon who urged me to look puzzled and say I didn't recall meeting him, and my Granny Willa who thought he looked vulnerable and wanted me to hug him, had paralyzed my vocal chords.

". . . this morning," he said, lifting his upper lip to show his perfect teeth in the way a Victorian lady would lift her skirt to give a man a glimpse of her ankle.

"Right, ah . . . ?"

"Dirk Koenig."

"Right." I tried to straighten up to resume my watch for the bus.

"May I give you a ride?"

Well, hot dang. After his abrupt dismissal of me in the bakeshop, he thought exposing expensive dental work and offering a ride in his six-figure car would make me eager to jump in.

The reality was, I was torn. This might be the one chance I'd have to ride in a car that cost more than what I'd earn in five years from my current jobs.

My inner Amazon whispered, *Reject the offer.* My nag chimed in with a warning about wrong men. My Granny Willa overruled them.

"Sure. Mitzi's Diner." I picked up my backpack.

"Hop in," he said and shifted back behind the wheel.

Okay, I'll admit I'm no better judge of men than Jade is, but even if Dirk was a wrong man, the odds of him being a serial killer were against his being a serial killer. Or were they? Something wasn't right about Dirk either—his calculating eyes and his sudden change of personality for starters. I paused with my hand on the door handle and peered inside. My eyes drifted over the buff-colored leather seats designed to fit the occupant like a glove, and they grazed over the gleaming dashboard studded with flashy dials and gadgets.

I unlatched the door and hopped in.

The purr of the motor and the scent of expensive leather enveloped me in the unfamiliar world of upscale luxury—a world where a car was more than transportation, it was a symbol of the owner's masculinity, regardless of their gender. The seat settled around me. I imagined myself owning a vehicle like this.

Dirk steered into the stream of traffic. My vibes merged with the car's power.

Dirk's honey-smooth voice broke my trance. "Are you having dinner at Mitzi's tonight?"

"Um, no. Working."

"At Mitzi's?"

"Temporarily. Until I find something better."

"Great food," he said.

Drats.

In Dirk's company, my insecurities sprang up like weeds, and I didn't have the right formula to banish them.

Dirk chuckled, took his right hand off the wheel and draped his free arm across the back of my seat. The beats of my heart pinged like the sound of hail hitting a tin roof.

Dirk punched something on the steering wheel. The volume of the music decreased.

He stopped for the signal and glanced at me. "When I was in high school, I spent hours on the weekends ogling the college girls who came into Mitzi's." The light changed. He turned the car onto West Sutton Street.

Dirk ogled college girls? My muscles tensed. I focused my attention on him. Even if he wasn't a killer, he may have another reason for luring me into his car. I edged closer to the door.

"The college crowd shows up at Mitzi's around nine most nights. Drop in some time. For old times' sake." The steadiness of my voice encouraged me. If Dirk had a dark side, I needed to keep fear out of my voice and keep a close watch on what he was doing.

Dirk laughed as he pulled to the curb in front of the diner. "Thanks, I may. Mitzi made the best chili I ever tasted and her milkshakes beat any I've had since."

"She still does and they still would," I said.

I leaned down to retrieve my backpack. His hand brushed the side of my head. The door of the glove compartment sprung open. Cold fear settled in the pit of my stomach, squeezed my heart, and constricted my lungs. I struggled to breathe as I ran my hand over the door panel to locate the handle and free myself from his car.

"Sorry," he said. He palmed an object he'd removed from the glove compartment. A gun? A knife? I couldn't tell.

Dirk stuck the fingers of his other hand into his shirt pocket. Did he keep the bullet for his gun in his shirt pocket like Barney Fife?

My nag admonished me. *This isn't funny, Agatha.* My right hand raced over the door panel, searching for the lever.

"I wanted to ask a favor," he said.

His voice carried a hint of sadness, a sound that always punches my compassion button. I leaned away from the side of the door and began to make a slow, methodical search for the door handle. Momma Dolly had been here for less than twenty-four hours and already my imagination was spinning innocent events into suspicious undertakings.

"Sure."

I watched as Dirk clicked the item he'd taken from the glove compartment and wrote something on a card he'd taken from his pocket.

"My cell phone number," he said thrusting the card toward me. "I have to leave town no later than tomorrow evening. I thought, since you stop in at the bakeshop everyday, you might be willing to check on my mother and then call me if she didn't look right."

"Is Gerda ill?" Showing concern for his mother was

a big plus in Dirk's favor. I turned my head to take another look at him as best I could in the dim light.

He stared straight ahead.

His profile was classic, a sculptor's dream.

"I don't know," he said.

His gaze appeared fixed on something far beyond the windshield.

"If I asked her, she wouldn't tell me. If I asked my dad, he wouldn't tell me either. But she's slowed down since the last time I was home."

"How long has it been since you were home?"

"A little over two years."

Maybe Dirk wasn't dangerous. But if he really cared about his parents, wouldn't he have visited them at least once a year? A day or two over the Christmas holidays shouldn't be too big a burden even for someone who worked hard and charged by the hour.

Unless he'd been incarcerated.

This new thought made sense—a realistic explanation for why it had been two years since he'd visited his parents and why he'd come home now. A lawyer convicted of a crime and sent to prison would lose his license to practice law. Maybe Gerda's Dirky wasn't so perfect after all. If I cared, Momma Dolly could find out the details of Dirk's downfall. I didn't.

"Sure, I'll be glad to check on your mother for you."

What was wrong with me? On this very day, I'd made a vow to avoid Koenig's Bake Shop. And now I'd agreed to do him a favor that would require me to visit the shop every day.

The sweet scents would stimulate my ultrasensitive

olfactory nerve. The beauty of their donuts would dazzle my eyes. Every morning, my willpower would be tested anew. Earning my daily gold star for healthy eating would be next to impossible.

"Thanks, ah, miss"—he turned and smiled at me— "may I call you Agatha?"

"Agatha's fine."

He was handsome, charming and rich. How could I not like him?

"I'll be gone for a week. Maybe a few days longer. But if you think there's a need, I can return earlier."

"—or Aggie, or Ags."

I tucked his card into my backpack. My right hand brushed something hard. The door handle. I pulled on the metal flange. The car door sprang open. "Thanks for the ride. May I call you Dirky?"

He laughed. "Sorry, Dirky is reserved for my mother. My friends call me Dirk."

"Then Dirk it is." I smiled. "There's an ink mark on your chin, Dirk."

He glanced at his chin in the rearview mirror but didn't rub it off. I admired his cool restraint.

"I'll compensate you for your time," he said opening his wallet. He looked at me. "Will fifty be enough?"

I stared into his eyes. "Your mother has been kind to me. I'm happy to return her kindness free of charge."

Did I appear needy—or mercenary?

I hustled out of his luxury car, slammed the door shut, and shrugged my backpack to my shoulder.

The passenger window lowered. "If you change your mind, my offer holds." He grinned like the Cheshire cat in *Alice in Wonderland.* The window zoomed upward. The sleek car roared away.

I wasn't surprised Dirk was the type who had to have the last word. I was surprised I'd agreed to do a favor for him. Part of the problem with my Granny Willa side was her reluctance to say no. My shoulders slumped and my eyes blurred as I walked around the outside of the diner to the service door.

How did a down-to-earth person like Gerda end up with a son who wore expensive dress shirts with a pair of jeans that had creases pressed into the legs—and who drove the hottest car on the market? How had a quiet, analytical introvert like me been born into a family of noisy, chaotic extroverts? It could only be because a hiccup in the universe jumbled the regular order.

By the time my shift ended, rain was falling with more force than the water out of my showerhead. The bandages I'd stuck over the sore places on my heels had worked loose. I counted my tips and summoned a taxi.

When the moonlight was obscured by the weather, the basement was pitch-black except for the glow of the furnace. I pulled out my keys, pushed the button on a tiny flashlight attached to the ring and got to my door without running into anything.

I listened. No sounds could be heard on the other side. I opened the door as quietly as I could.

The red digital numbers on the clock radio on the kitchen counter showed 11:32. A nightlight plugged into a wall socket added a feeble light. Momma Dolly, with a lilac nightcap covering the hair rollers on her head, was asleep on the couch. Miss Priss, mimicking Momma Dolly's light snores, was curled at her feet.

The television screen flickered, but no sound came from the speakers. I found the remote control on the side table and turned it off.

"Agatha?" Momma Dolly coughed and sat up. "I wanted to stay awake until you got back, but my long day caught up with me, and I couldn't keep my eyes open a second longer."

"Hi." I said. "Let me get my pj's and use the bathroom and then you take the bedroom. The temp agency hasn't scheduled me for tomorrow. We can spend the day together and talk."

"No need to give up your bed, Agatha. Miss Priss and I are fine on the couch."

"If your back goes out, we can't shop or dine out or explore the city. Instead of having fun, I'll be applying liniment to your back and listening to you groan."

She dropped her protest about sleeping in my bed.

I put on an old pair of pajamas and washed my face and brushed my teeth.

When I returned to the living area, Momma Dolly stood up, stretched and without another word hobbled off toward the bedroom.

She never wanted to let on that sometimes her bones ached and her feet hurt. She didn't want anyone to mention her age or celebrate her birthday. But the wear and tear from a life lived in a state of self-created emotional turmoil and in a constant swirl of physical motion had taken a toll—even if she didn't talk about it.

I adjusted my body around the lumps in my couch

and drifted into a state of contentment. For the first time, since moving to Millerton where I knew no one and no one knew me, I felt secure.

My Momma Dolly was asleep in the next room.

Chapter Five

Early the next morning Momma Dolly and I sat at my forties–era table eating the bran flakes and milk she'd bought at the grocery last night.

She refilled her bowl and picked up the milk carton. "So what do you do in your free time?"

Nothing I wanted to share. Any mention of my plan to make over my personality would result in my being peppered with a flurry of questions about why, when, and how I'd ever thought up such a foolish thing.

"I see you found a grocery store," I said, tilting my bowl and spooning up the last of the milk.

"And such a grocery store—case after case of pre-pared foods and fruit as pretty as the waxed fruit in the blue pottery bowl on my kitchen counter."

Her bowl of wax fruit had been on her kitchen counter as long as I could remember.

"Every time you pretended to bite into a piece of the

wax fruit, Christy and I burst out laughing. We always believed you forgot the fruit wasn't real."

"We've had some good laughs over the years."

I nodded.

"The pear, with the rosy spot on the green-speckled skin, was always my favorite," I said.

I picked up the milk carton Momma Dolly had set back on the table to read the words on the front. My suspicion was confirmed. The carton contained a combination of cream and milk in equal proportions. Whole milk and cream were not on my list of healthy foods. Ingesting this much fat could disqualify me from earning today's star. I shrugged, filled my bowl with more flakes and poured. The bran should make up for the additional fat.

"Those were the days, Agatha. We had fun didn't we?"

"Lots."

Momma Dolly stopped her spoon in midair and gazed into space. "My fun days are over."

Her voice was full of woe. I studied her face. She didn't look sick. Her color was good. Her eyes sparkled. She had the energy, even after her long drive yesterday, to walk to the grocery.

"Doctor Mimms gave you bad news at your last checkup," I said.

"What?"

"You have an incurable disease." My voice wobbled, making me sound as panicked as I felt.

Momma Dolly got up from the table, picked up her cereal bowl and carried it to the sink. She rinsed the bowl and spoon, and stacked them in the dish drainer.

My brain was in a free fall. I couldn't eat another bite. Momma Dolly had come to visit me before . . .

"It's my heart, Agatha."

"Congestive heart failure," I blurted.

"What?"

"Heart failure."

"Who?"

"You."

"Not me. Doctor Mimms said I have the heart of a forty-year-old athlete."

"Then why did you say your fun days are over?"

"I cannot marry Herman. He refused to sign a prenuptial agreement."

So this was the reason she'd showed up here. The wanton killing of birds by Miss Priss was a side issue.

"Why—"

Momma Dolly gushed out her pent up sorrow. "Herman said signing a prenuptial agreement is insulting—a sign I don't trust him. He says he doesn't need or want my money; and, since he has no children, anything of his is mine anyway."

"—won't you marry him without one?"

For a moment her lips clamped shut and her eyelids lowered. "I can't, Agatha. It's complicated."

Momma Dolly sat down, laid her forearms on the table and looked at me with the saddest expression I'd ever seen on her face.

"I trusted my second husband, Agatha. It turned out to be the biggest mistake of my life. He talked so sweet but he was a scoundrel of the worst sort."

Momma Dolly paused and started shredding a paper

napkin. When she looked at me again, her eyes begged for understanding.

"When we returned from our honeymoon, I was in a stupor. My second husband was agile. He told me he had a degree in accounting so when he insisted on taking over the job of paying the bills, I didn't put up a fight. By the time I learned the mortgage hadn't been paid for six months, he'd cleaned out our joint bank account and taken off for Nevada with Bunny Warner. Since then, I've insisted on a signed prenuptial agreement before I marry. And I no longer open a joint bank account."

Momma Dolly never talked about her money. She was a committed bargain hunter, but she always had enough to do and buy whatever she wanted.

"So, because your second husband ran off with your money and your friend and left you with nothing to sustain you but a bowl of wax fruit, you don't trust Herman." I raised my eyebrows and lowered my jaw in mock horror.

"Agatha Marple, missy . . ." Momma Dolly sputtered and planted her fists at her waist. She skewered me with her you're-getting-too-big-for-your-britches look. "Moving here and living alone hasn't been good for you, Agatha. You've developed a sarcastic tone and a sassy attitude."

"Living alone changes people."

"Does it? I wouldn't know." Her eyes brightened. "I've always lived with someone, even between my marriages."

"If you want, I'll show you a super thrift shop in the

neighborhood. Once you get inside, you'll forget about all of your current and past troubles."

Momma Dolly's face lit up at the prospect of searching through a new thrift shop.

"Let me open a can of cat food and put some in a bowl for Miss Priss first."

"Sure."

As we rode the service elevator to the lobby, I considered our route. Unless we walked an extra mile, the shortest way to the thrift shop went past Koenig's. I figured with Momma Dolly setting a good pace, I would be fine if I held my breath in the vicinity of Koenig's.

Harold opened the building's door for Momma Dolly. I managed to squeeze through before it closed.

She gave him a warm smile. "You look very professional this morning, Harold."

"Thank you, Mrs. McWater."

We hurried along the sidewalk.

"Did you notice the color of Harold's eyes, Agatha? Like blue sapphires. Maybe you haven't married yet because you expect too much from a man."

I wasn't going to confide in her that I was no longer interested in getting married. Nor that my spare energy was concentrated on my becoming a strong independent woman whose life was complete without a man.

"Is expecting one's fiancé not to cheat too much to ask?"

"You and Jake weren't married," Momma Dolly said as though the fact that Jake and I were only engaged made his being unfaithful okay.

"Well, the only men I'll consider marrying are men who are rich enough to buy me an apartment in Paris and a penthouse in Manhattan. And that eliminates Harold."

Momma Dolly laughed. "I taught you well, Agatha. But there comes a time—" She came to an abrupt halt. We were in front of Koenig's Bake Shop. Momma Dolly sniffed. "You're thirty-two and three and three-quarter months old, Agatha."

"And I'm smart enough to avoid being the bride in a wedding that has the word divorce spelled out in neon letters above the altar."

Momma Dolly huffed. But her attention was directed to the window of Koenig's.

I felt a burst of encouragement. Sticking up for myself with Momma Dolly was a new experience for me. I could respond to her overbearing advice with words instead of shutting myself in my room and locking the door.

Momma Dolly cupped her hands around her eyes and peered through the shop window. "I'm going to run in to see if they have a loaf of rye."

"Not a good idea."

"Why?"

"I'm not stopping here."

"Why?"

"I have issues with their donuts."

"I don't doubt it. Your grandfather had trouble with donuts too. Anything fried upset his stomach something awful. Wait out here for me. I'll only be a minute."

The door of the shop creaked open. Dirk Koenig stared at me. "Miss Marple."

He surveyed Momma Dolly who had chosen to wear

a red tank top and a turquoise gypsy skirt today. "My grandmother, Mrs. McWater, Mr. Koenig."

"Mrs. McWater." Dirk nodded to her. But rather than taking a step forward he retreated back inside. My grandmother started into the shop. She tripped on the threshold, moaned, and clutched her chest.

Dirk's eagle eyes turned into owl eyes. He took Momma Dolly's elbow and guided her toward a chair, asking several times if she was okay. I imagined his lawyer's brain calculating the cost to the shop if my grandmother sued.

But I knew she was faking. Pretending to trip or to slip were ploys she used to draw attention to herself. Her daughter, my mother, worked as an actress, but it was my grandmother who had the real acting talent in the family.

Momma Dolly inhaled several deep breaths and fluttered a hand over the center of her chest. She declared she was fine but kept a pained grimace on her face.

Dirk pulled out a chair for her. She eased herself down.

"Fresh baking—such a wonderful smell," she said in a voice contrived to sound as though she was fighting to catch her breath. "You must be proud of your establishment, Mr. Koenig."

"My parents' establishment, Mrs. McWater."

Dirk sat across from her. He smiled, flashing his pearly teeth at her.

In return, Momma Dolly gave him a wavering smile and tried beguiling him with her own endearing tricks.

I felt awkward and intrusive standing over them. I turned to study the contents of the display case.

The door to the back swung open.

"Oh Chicky, I didn't know we had customers," Gerda said. "The bell didn't jangle."

She wiped her hands on her apron and tilted her head to look around me.

"Dirky? I thought you were going out?"

I was trapped in the middle of a conversation again. I dashed for the shop's unisex bathroom.

Out of the corner of my eye, I saw Momma Dolly get to her feet. I turned back. Dirk jumped up from his chair. A look of horror contorted his face. He reached out to grab Momma Dolly. "Mrs. McWater, please sit down. I'll be happy to get whatever you need."

Momma Dolly evaded him like a football running back and rushed toward Gerda.

I changed direction and joined Dirk, who was looking concerned.

"Don't worry about my grandmother. She loves to divert one's attention by creating a sense of drama."

"What was your grandmother diverting attention from?"

"She wanted you to hang around for a while."

"For what purpose?"

"To determine if you should be considered a good prospect."

Dirk laughed.

I giggled.

"What do you think she's decided?" he asked.

"I won't know until she's ready to advise me to consider you."

He gazed at me with an intense look—a disconcerting look.

I think I blushed. But I didn't turn away or lower my eyes.

Momma Dolly closed in on the sale counter. "What a beautiful accent you have," Momma Dolly said to Gerda. "I thought, from the name, I could get a proper loaf of rye bread here. My second husband introduced me to many things, and German rye bread was one of them."

I didn't want to think about the other things the scoundrel who'd run off with her money and her friend had introduced her to. But at least she'd gotten something of value from having been married to him.

"Tomorrow. Mrs . . . ?"

"McWater, Dolly McWater."

"Tomorrow is rye bread. Today is pumpernickel."

"Then I'll be back tomorrow." She examined the cakes in the glass case. "Today I'll have a piece of this chocolate cake," she said pointing her finger at her selection, "and coffee."

A soft groan resisted my effort to contain it. Dirk smiled at me and hurried out the front door.

"Bye Dirky," Gerda called as the door swung closed. "And you, Chicky? What can Gerda serve you today?"

"A cup of coffee. Decaf."

She hesitated. Her eyes probed my defenses for a weak spot. "You are sure?"

"I'm sure."

I heard the familiar tsk-tsk clicks of her tongue as

she bent down to retrieve a chocolate-frosted, three-layer cake from the case.

Momma Dolly and I sat. Gerda brought the coffees and a large slice of the cake.

"Won't you join us, Mrs. Koenig?" Momma Dolly asked.

To my surprise, Gerda took a chair from the next table and sat with us.

Momma Dolly added sugar to her coffee. "Such a handsome and considerate son you're blessed with, Mrs. Koenig. You must be proud to have such a boy. I have a daughter and two granddaughters." Momma Dolly picked up her fork.

"I have two boys. My Dirky, who you met, and Gunter are both good boys, but I'm sad for no daughter."

"They work here? At the bakeshop? Your boys?"

"No. No. Gunter is an airline pilot and Dirky is . . . was a lawyer."

"Well, I suppose you have daughters-in-laws to enjoy."

"Unfortunately, I do not."

Momma Dolly maintained a poker player's face as she took in this important information.

"This chocolate cake is the best I've eaten in all my years. And, if I might mention this—without sounding as if I am boasting—I make a prize-winning chocolate cake myself. Two-time blue ribbon winner at the state fair—Fifty-eight and Fifty-nine."

Gerda beamed and nodded at Momma Dolly. "Mr. Koenig uses only the best quality ingredients for his baking." She turned her gaze and glared at me. "Everything he makes is healthy."

"Yes," Momma Dolly said. "A discerning palate can tell right off only high quality ingredients were used to create this cake. Do you share recipes, Mrs. Koenig?"

Gerda lowered her eyes. "I'm sorry, Mrs. McWater."

"Very smart of you. A successful businessperson guards their secrets." Momma Dolly wiped her lips and beamed at Gerda.

Gerda got to her feet and moved her chair back to its original spot. "A pleasure to meet you, Mrs. McWater. I hope to have you as a regular customer of our bakeshop during your visit like our Chicky. And if you bake one of your prize-winning cakes while you're here, I would enjoy tasting it."

"Chicky?" Momma Dolly looked around. "Who's Chicky?"

"Your granddaughter." Gerda chortled and pointed at me. "I call her Chicky because one day when she came in for her donut she had a feathery, yellow scarf around her neck. She looked like a baby chick."

My eyelids flew upwards. I'd never figured out why Gerda had started to call me Chicky. I thought the nickname might be an endearment she used for all of her young female customers. Tomorrow that feathery, yellow scarf would be in the donation box of a local charity. I'd search the thrift shops for a replacement. A silky cheetah or leopard print would better reflect my budding Amazon personality.

Momma Dolly laughed. "Dirky and Chicky," she said.

I eyed Momma Dolly as if she was a spider who'd dropped down from the ceiling. *Little Miss Muffet sat on her tuffet . . .*

"We really must be going," I said, fixing her with what I hoped was a look that would silence her and get her to move.

She folded her paper napkin and placed it neatly in the center of her plate. Her knees creaked as she got to her feet.

"I'm so glad to have met you, Mrs. Koenig. What a delight to discover an excellent bakery close to the place I'm staying."

"My pleasure meeting you, Mrs. McWater. I'll put aside tomorrow's best loaf of rye bread for you."

My head throbbed with a dull pain. I gave a gentle push to Momma Dolly's elbow to get her to move.

Dirky and Chicky. Ha. Never in a millennium.

Chapter Six

I opened the door of the thrift shop. The clang of the bell over the door caused the clerk sitting behind the counter to glance up. She greeted us and returned to her book.

Momma Dolly's eyes took on a feral gleam as she surveyed a bargain hunter's paradise.

"Look Agatha," she said, picking up an item from the nearest table. "This purse still has the original price tag attached." She turned the tag over. "Fifty-nine dollars." She placed it back on the table and shook her head. "Can you imagine? Someone paid fifty-nine dollars for a purse and then never used it."

"Maybe it was a gift and the person who gave it left the price tag on." I picked up the purse and turned it around—checking it from every angle. I unzipped it and looked inside. "Nice. It's got a toggle in here to hold your keys. You think Mom would like it?"

"A chartreuse purse with pink shells sewn on is hard to work into a wardrobe, Agatha. There's a reason it ended up here unused."

"Mom loves bright colors."

"Being made of straw limits its usefulness."

I put the purse down. Momma Dolly was an expert at creating colorful ensembles. I would trust her about the purse.

We worked our way around the table.

"If I find a nice set of dishes at a good price, I'll consider buying them," I mused aloud as we wandered deeper into the store.

Momma Dolly stopped near the second-hand furniture display and scanned the layout. "You go look at the dishes. I'll look around on my own and meet you back here in thirty minutes."

She headed in the direction of the case that displayed the second-hand jewelry. I wound my way through the crowded aisles to the house wares area.

Several full sets of dishes and numerous odd pieces from incomplete sets covered three long shelves. I took up a plate with a dainty flower bouquet decorating the center and a thin band of gold trim circling the edge. Not bad. But I wanted plain dishes. Something nice but suited for everyday use. My apartment had a two-burner stove with an oven that wasn't much bigger than the Bake-It-Now oven I got as a gift for my seventh birthday—the one with the tiny pans and the packaged mixes that produce an edible product. Cooking elaborate meals in tight quarters was impossible. I pretty much stuck to fixing one-pot dinners.

I looked through the three shelves but didn't find a set of dishes I wanted to buy.

I moved on and sorted through the racks of clothes. I took a sleeveless black dress and a nice gray pantsuit that would be perfect when I had a professional job, to the curtained off try-on area.

Keeping my back to the mirror that covered a large section of the institutional-green cinderblock wall, I removed my outer clothes and slipped on the dress before turning around to look.

The silky fabric draped my hips with no wrinkles. The V-neckline flattered my round face. A keeper. The pantsuit also fit fine. The shade of gray didn't make me look as if I'd been drained of blood. Priced at seven dollars and ninety-five cents, the pantsuit was a keeper too.

"Agatha?"

The face of Momma Dolly filled a small parting between the curtains.

"Here I am," I said as I sucked in my stomach to pull up the zipper of my jeans.

"I didn't see you on the floor. I wondered where you got to," she said adding a huff at the end.

I held up the dress and suit. "I wanted to try these on before deciding. Sorry, I should've let you know."

"Well, I thought you'd forgotten me and left."

Momma Dolly was not a person one could forget— not even if one wanted to.

I noted the hint of wistful irritation in her voice. Her way of letting me know she wanted concern shown. "I'm sorry," I said.

She stepped into the fitting area.

"The clerk at the jewelry counter was talking about her daughter's divorce. She's a wreck over the whole affair—the clerk, not her daughter. She likes her son-in-law better than she likes her daughter and thinks she'll never see him again."

"That could cause someone trouble."

"Her daughter doesn't plan to be friends with her ex like so many of today's couples. She informed her mother she isn't allowed to invite him to family get-togethers."

"I doubt her ex-son-in-law would be a good prospect for me to consider—if that's what you're thinking."

Momma Dolly took the black dress from me and held it up in front of her and studied herself in the mirror.

"I really should get something in this color."

"Why? You never wear black. Red is your choice for funerals and all other special occasions."

"I should get a black dress to wear in case I'm foolish enough to marry again." Momma Dolly chortled as she handed me back the dress.

"Now that you know about this thrift shop, you can stop in often and check out the dresses in your size. A nice black dress, suitable for a wedding, could come in at any time," I said.

"I think I will. Mrs. Butner, Lilly, the sales clerk, could use my counsel as she deals with the loss of her son-in-law. And, on the way here, I could stop at the bake shop and say hello to Mrs. Koenig."

What counsel she could offer to Mrs. Butner, I couldn't imagine. With the exception of Momma Dolly's second husband, all of her living ex-husbands and all of my mother's ex's, including my father, showed up for every holiday and came to our family reunion every year.

We caught the bus to the mall on the outskirts of town to have lunch in the cafeteria.

"I really like this town, Agatha—such pleasant people, the most wonderful shops, good bus service and a cafeteria."

"It's nice here, but not as nice as home where you know everyone and where your yearly social calendar is set," I said.

She stopped reading the bus schedule the driver had given her and eyed me over the top of her reading glasses. "You'll be moving home then?"

"Well, no. At least not right away. I'm giving myself more time to find a good job. Six months at least."

"I had an appointment with your ex-boss Mr. Jeeter at his law office to get advice on the prenup. He said he'd be happy to take you back if you want to come home. And you don't have to worry about Jake bothering you. He's marrying Sally . . . ah . . . what's her name . . . next Saturday."

"Benton?"

"That's the one. Glen Benton's daughter, skinny gal with buck teeth and a sloping chin. I hinted to Glen several times about the wonders of braces. He never took the hint."

My emotional platform rocked. After all the years Jake and I had been together, he might have had the decency to wait a few months before showing his true colors.

I poked my upper teeth over my lower lip. "Look what braces did for me," I said.

Momma Dolly giggled. I laughed, but inside I was melting. My world had turned wobbly as if it had been knocked off its pivot point.

How could Jake marry Sally Benton when he could have married me? My teeth were straight, my bite did not overlap. I had a strong chin. Maybe I was willful and even strident at times but our children wouldn't have needed expensive braces and chin implants. And then a reasonable explanation for his marrying her came to me. She didn't care if Jake was a two–timing louse.

When we got back to the apartment, I stayed under my pitiful shower for a long time. I knew I was prettier and nicer than Sally Benton and a lot smarter too. Maybe that's why Jake hadn't been faithful to me. He couldn't marry someone he didn't feel superior to. And so he wouldn't be blamed for the breakup, as he'd cheated on me until I'd had enough.

My heart went out to Sally. She was a sweet person who didn't deserve the heartbreak Jake would give her.

By the time I got out of the shower and dried off, my mood was on the rise. I gave a silent thanks to the last person who'd ratted on Jake.

I could smell dinner cooking. I walked into the front room. Momma Dolly was busy at the stove. Enthroned on my beanbag chair, Miss Priss was grooming herself.

My world was back in balance.

I picked up Miss Priss, folded myself into the beanbag and flicked on the television.

Chapter Seven

In the morning, I left early to make my promised daily check on Gerda. I covered the distance to the bakeshop in record time.

"Chicky, you're early."

I peered into Gerda's eyes. They were as bright and lively as ever. Her cheeks were rosy. Nothing that I could detect was wrong. There was no need to call Dirky.

"A plain donut to go," I said before I could stop myself.

Today, through the temp agency, I was working at the headquarters of Alldisaster Insurance for the third time. I loved Alldisaster. They had an employee cafeteria with great food at fair prices, a pleasant coffee shop on the ground floor where the workers gathered before the start of the workday and on their breaks, an exercise room, super benefits, and every three months or so they brought in motivational speakers to give free lectures to their employees. It was a company that had the potential for advancement. If they offered me a permanent job, I would take it.

I joined the crowd waiting for an empty slot in the revolving door and checked my watch—fifteen minutes before I was due at the office of a Mr. Tideman.

I sat at the desk in the front office. Mr. Tideman never came out of his office. At nine, he rang the phone and told me not to disturb him. If anyone called or came in, I was to take a message.

By the time the workday ended I was drained from eight hours of doing nothing. I stepped off the bus and walked the short distance to my apartment building. No doorman was at the door. I entered the lobby and rang for the service elevator.

The floor indicator for the elevator showed B and then L. The doors opened. I punched B. The elevator descended. The doors parted to frame Momma Dolly, who grinned at me. She started talking before I could get out of the elevator.

I sighed.

Momma Dolly glowed. Her hands conducted her words, and her eyes danced. "That darling Harold buzzed me to let me know you were home."

Harold should be brought up on charges for deserting his post.

"So, that's why Harold wasn't at the door. I thought he'd been—"

"Isn't he the sweetest, most considerate young man? He'll make some lucky woman a wonderful husband." Momma Dolly's eyes stopped dancing and studied me.

I scrunched up my nose. "—fired."

"Fired?"

"Replaced. Let go. Why were you so eager to know the minute I got home anyway?"

"Because I'm bursting with good news." Momma Dolly threaded her arm through mine as we walked through the rattling, hissing basement to my apartment.

Had she patched up her quarrel with Mr. Dent? Was she going home in the morning? I crossed the fingers on my free hand. And sent out my wish to the place where wishes go to be fulfilled.

She squeezed my arm. "I took Miss Priss to the vet for a checkup. The vet, by the way, is a very handsome man and impressive in his white coat. Sad to say, he was wearing a wedding ring."

"Then I won't consider him a good prospect."

Momma Dolly ignored my comment. "After he checked Miss Priss, he assured me eating wild birds hadn't damaged her."

"Birds are a natural diet for cats—mice too."

"More like a hundred birds, I told him. And the harm done to the birds wasn't mentioned."

"When cats are around, birds must be vigilant."

"Thank you, Agatha. That's exactly what Herman does not understand. The birds in his neighborhood cannot relax for fear of being stalked by his cat. I told Herman, several times, Miss Priss isn't an alley cat who has to hunt to eat. She's a pampered pet whose natural diet comes from a box or a can."

"What else kept you busy today?" I asked turning the knob on the apartment door.

"I picked up the loaf of rye bread from the bakery

and had a nice visit with Mrs. Koenig. That darling Mr. Koenig came in and asked about you."

"Gerda's husband asked about me?"

"No, Dark."

"Dirk. His name's Dirk." He'd told me he'd be leaving town last night. Maybe Gerda is sick. "What exactly did Dirk say?"

"He asked how your exercise program was going."

"My exercise program?"

"I told him I didn't think you had an exercise program. He laughed. A very nice laugh. A sweet laugh. A laugh one could enjoy hearing forever. And then he said the first time he saw you, you were wearing exercise clothes."

"Do not say another word to Dirk Koenig about me or about him to me."

"Why?"

"Because, he's a wrong man. And, unlike Jade, I've learned my lesson about wrong men."

"Well, fine, I told him you got all A's in school." Momma Dolly huffed.

I put an arm around her shoulders. "The truth is, besides the temptation of Koenig's donuts, Dirk is the other reason I am staying away from the bakeshop."

She did not comment, nor say a word about considering Dirk a good prospect.

I stepped into the apartment. The savory smell of sausages and sauerkraut greeted me.

"After dinner, if you aren't too tired, we can go to the diner where I work and have coffee. I can introduce you to my coworkers and to Mitzi, the owner."

"I have plenty of energy left—even after the work it took to get this nice meal together." Momma Dolly lifted the lid on the skillet. "Wash up. I'll fix our plates."

When I came back, Momma Dolly was seated at the table spreading mustard on a piece of sausage. A white dinner plate with a simple basket weave design around the rim, sat at my place. The center of the plate held a sausage atop a mound of sauerkraut and three boiled redskin potatoes.

"Where did you find these dishes?" I asked as I sat down.

"The gracious lobby hostess, Mrs. Simmons, has permission to dispose of things after sixty days. These were left in a vacated apartment three months ago by a previous tenant. She'd planned on donating them to her church charity sale. But, as soon as I saw them, I offered to buy them on the spot."

"They're perfect."

Momma Dolly beamed. "There's a full set for eight, no chips or cracks. But, if you don't like them, there's still time to donate them to the charity sale."

"I like them." I cut a piece off a portion of sausage. "You knew I would."

"They're plain like you like." Momma Dolly concentrated on eating for a while and spread more mustard on her remaining piece of sausage. "Mrs. Simmons offered us extra storage space at no increased charge."

"Why?"

"Agatha, you should know to trust me."

I'd spent years patching up Momma Dolly's misunderstandings with other people. My grandmother often failed to get many of the details straight. I'd check with Mrs. Simmons about how free this storage space was before I moved anything into it.

After dinner we set out for Mitzi's.

"I love diners," Momma Dolly said as we went up the steps. I pulled open the front door and stepped aside for her to enter. "Almost as much as I love cafeterias."

Her nose twitched and her gaze roamed the interior. She leaned toward me, cupped a hand around her mouth, and whispered in my ear, "Agatha, look?" She pointed toward the back of the diner. Before I could stop her, she was waving and weaving her way around the tables toward the rear. Her five thin bracelets jangled.

My eyes lit up. I would buy a collar with a bell for Miss Priss. The birds in Mr. Dent's neighborhood would no longer be in peril. Momma Dolly could go home.

As she headed to the booth Dirk Koenig occupied, she toppled several of the salt and pepper shakers on the tables she passed.

I righted the shakers Momma Dolly had knocked over as I dragged myself along the path she'd forged.

I didn't want to spend time with Dirk. Not here, not anywhere. After saying he would be leaving town and then getting me to agree to do him a favor, he hadn't left. Had he asked me to check on Gerda to trick me into going into the bakery?

My emotions tumbled over like the salt and pepper shakers.

Dirk stood when Momma Dolly neared. His smile looked genuine. He greeted her and gestured for her to slide into the bench seat across from him.

Momma Dolly slipped in the wall, leaving space for me.

"Hi, Agatha," Dirk said. "I got held up. I'm leaving tomorrow."

"Okay."

Momma Dolly looked up from the menu and gave me a quick glance.

I focused my gaze on Mitzi's menu even though I knew her menu by heart. Della, our waitress, came to take our order. Momma Dolly ordered tea. I ordered coffee.

Putting aside the menu, I kept my eyes centered on a napkin-wrapped bundle of silverware—moving it from one hand to the other.

. . . and the dish ran away with the spoon.

Momma Dolly went into her information-gathering mode.

"Your mother told me you practice corporate law, Mr. Koenig."

"I did."

"I see. And what career are you pursuing now?"

"I'm considering a lot of different options."

"No need to rush into a decision, I suppose."

"Mom and Pop are glad to have me here. Until they tire of me being around, I can take my time."

Della set a metal teapot along with a cup and my cup of coffee on the table. Momma Dolly poured tea and ripped open a packet of real sugar into her cup.

"Hmm." Momma Dolly stirred her tea. "Are you re-locating to Millerton then?"

"I may. If things work out."

"I'm considering moving here myself." Momma Dolly tucked a wayward strand of hair behind her ear.

My heart dropped into a dark abyss. I took a sip of coffee. It went down wrong. I coughed. The cup rattled as I sat it back in the saucer.

Dirk raised his eyebrows.

"How is your mother, Mr. Koenig?" I asked.

Thank goodness, my voice didn't shake like my cup.

"Dirk," he said. "She isn't coughing," he added and winked at me.

Momma Dolly grabbed another packet of sugar to dump into her cup.

His wink had unbalanced me again. I slid out of the booth. "Let me see if there's any of Mitzi's lemon meringue pie left." I assumed my waitress persona. "May I get something for you, Dirk?" I looked straight at him.

"Thanks, but Della's doing a good job."

Suspicious is the nature of lawyers I think. And assigning criminal motives to the innocent actions of innocent people could be a job hazard. But would Dirk think my offer to get something for him was meant to imply Della wasn't doing a good job?

I turned on my heel and went to get a slice of lemon meringue pie for Momma Dolly. Mitzi stopped me and asked how Momma Dolly and I were getting along and when Momma Dolly would be going home.

By the time I returned to the table, Momma Dolly was patting Dirk's hand. He excused himself, slid out of the booth, picked up both bills and hurried off.

The sorrowful expression in his eyes tugged at my heart.

I sat down in Dirk's vacated seat, faced Momma Dolly, and waited for her to explain. She dug the edge of her fork through the mound of brown-tinged fluffy white topping, through the shimmering yellow layer below and through the flakey crust. "Perfect."

She put the forkful of pie into her mouth. "Delicious."

She said nothing about the intimate scene I'd witnessed between her and Dirk.

I rested my elbows on the table, turned the palms of my hands up and spread my hands apart. "So?"

"So what?"

"So why were you offering solace to Mrs. Koenig's son?"

"The final papers dissolving his marriage came today."

"Oh." Something inside of me brightened.

"Don't expect me to reveal any more of Dirk's confidences."

"Fine. I don't care to know anything about his personal life. I thought he was upset about Gerda."

"Why?"

"It's a long story." I changed the subject. "I'm thinking of moving, somewhere far from Koenig's bakeshop. Closer to Mitzi's, I think."

Momma Dolly shook her fork at me and scowled. "You should know by now running away solves nothing."

My surprise at hearing this coming from her caused me to sputter. "How can you say that to me after you kidnapped Mr. Dent's cat and ran away from him?"

"My situation is different than yours, Agatha."

"How?"

"I'm clear about what I'm doing."

"Then our situations aren't different. I'm clear about what I'm doing. Jake was a louse. He insisted on having his own way about everything. He never considered what would make me happy. And, the sad thing is, I let him get away with his boorish behavior far too long. But now I'm free, and I'm working on asserting myself, stating my needs, and doing what pleases me."

Momma Dolly finished her pie and looked me square in the eye. "You know you get your stubborn streak from me."

"I know. Let's go home. I have to work tomorrow."

The next morning, I was in front of Koenig's bakery when Dirk's car came around the corner. I waved, hoping he would see me. My Granny Willa side wanted him to know I was keeping my promise to check on his mother.

I opened the door to the bakeshop.

"Hi, Chicky. Dirky left a few minutes ago," Gerda said.

"I saw his car go past."

"How you know Dirky's car?"

"He saw me waiting for the bus the other evening and offered me a ride."

"Such a considerate boy, my Dirky. So which donut for you today, Chicky?"

Gerda looked and sounded fine today. "No donut. A decaf coffee. To go. I'm following my new life plan."

"If that's what you want, Chicky, Gerda is saying nothing more about such foolishness."

She didn't have to say anything. The scowl on her face made it clear how she felt. I picked up the filled cardboard container. "Thanks Gerda. See you tomorrow."

"Tomorrow Koenig's is having a special—extra nuts on the frosted donuts at the regular price."

Great. Gerda had upped the level of temptation.

And I had committed myself to show up here tomorrow to check on her.

When I got home from work, Momma Dolly was cooking.

Over dinner, she dropped her latest news.

"Tomorrow, I'll be moving some things into our extra storage space. Harold volunteered his help."

What things? I was too tired and too fearful of the answer to ask the question.

"Okay," I said, sounding as flat as my mood.

I finished eating and headed to the medicine cabinet. I took out the bottle of extra-strength headache pills and swallowed two.

Chapter Eight

The independence I'd gained from running away was gone. Each day, Momma Dolly rooted herself deeper into my sanctuary. And, in her usual fashion, she had reordered things in a manner that pleased her.

And maybe I didn't care anymore.

Living in a town where everyone was a stranger had been lonely. Being on my own, with no one to care if I came home or didn't, had been scary.

Enthralled in Momma Dolly's orbit—a place where the center was in constant motion—I felt safe. And I'd maintained a few boundaries and had stuck up for me—whichever *me* was in charge at the time—on occasion.

But until I abandoned my efforts to elevate my Amazon side and conceded the upper hand to Granny Willa, there was hope.

*   *   *

I made my check on Gerda before going to work. She looked fine. I purchased two bran muffins for Momma Dolly and hurried back to the apartment.

There was no sign Momma Dolly was awake. I left the bakery bag on the table and headed for the bus stop to catch the seven-forty-five bus.

I took the nearest empty seat, took out my cell phone and called my apartment phone.

No answer.

At Alldisaster, I was informed Mr. Tideman no longer worked there. I was reassigned to the data entry department for the rest of the week.

A happy change of circumstance. There was always plenty of work to do there. At lunch, I sat in the cafeteria with the remains of a tuna salad sandwich in front of me and tried to reach Momma Dolly again—and got no answer. My heartbeat began marching to "Triumph of Time," one of John Philip Sousa's compositions with the flourishing snare drums and clashing cymbals.

My left eye twitched. Momma Dolly hadn't stirred when I was getting ready for work, I didn't see or hear her when I'd returned with the bran muffins, and she hadn't answered my earlier call.

I called the front desk.

"Mrs. Simmons," said the musical voice of the building manager.

"Mrs. Simmons, Agatha Marple. Have you seen my grandmother this morning?"

"I have. She brought coffee and two delicious and helpful bran muffins to share with me an hour ago. And then she went out."

"Thanks. If you see her, don't mention I called. I'll talk to her when I get home."

"Your grandmother has a busy day ahead of her, Miss Marple."

Momma Dolly's days were always busy. Now that I knew she wasn't lying in her bed too sick to get up, I could stop worrying. I said good-bye, hung up and headed back to the data entry department. I would learn the details of her busy day soon enough.

After work, I hopped off the bus three stops before my regular stop. I needed some exercise after spending eight hours sitting in front of a computer. My route took me past Koenig's. I couldn't resist looking in the window.

My mouth dropped open. I blinked twice. Momma Dolly was behind Koenig's sale counter with a Koenig's apron on. I went in, marched to the front of the counter and took the same fighter's stance I'd taken in Jolly's Café.

Momma Dolly had moved into my apartment, gave no date for when she planned to leave, arranged for more storage space for what purpose I didn't know, and now she'd taken a job.

I glared and pointed a finger at her. "What are you doing?" My voice must have been a little loud.

She put her fingers over her lips and nodded at a customer, sitting at the window table. "I'm working, Agatha."

I lowered the tone of my voice. "Why? You haven't worked at a job in twenty years."

"Gerda wanted to attend the funeral of an old friend

and rather than asking Hans to take over at the counter for her, she offered to hire me on part-time."

Her words confirmed what I suspected, she wasn't leaving. "So what time will you be home for dinner?"

"I get off at six."

"Is pizza okay?" I leaned over the glass top of the counter and examined the contents of the display case below.

"Pizza's fine."

I hustled out of the shop to put some distance between me and the last éclair.

I walked to Joe's Pizza Place and placed an order for a pepperoni with extra cheese. Nutritionists say pizza is a complete meal but I needed something that had fewer calories. I went a couple of blocks out of my way to purchase greens and a cucumber for a salad, picked up the pizza, and headed home.

When I got back to the apartment, I pulled out the salad items and set them on the counter. I put the vanilla ice cream I'd added to my basket in the freezer and stored the four cans of tomato soup.

Keeping busy was good. It kept me from thinking too much.

I fixed the salad and headed into the bedroom to change out of my work clothes.

And froze. My double bed was gone. In its place were two twin beds. A new armoire stood against the far wall. I stared at the evidence that proved I had lost control of my space.

My inner Amazon shriveled. My nag remained

silent. Granny Willa had gone into hiding. All that was left was an urge to scream.

To avoid collapsing into a non-functioning heap, I went into the kitchen area, took everything out of the cupboards, washed the shelves, then put everything back in place. I scrubbed the tile floor. I polished the appliances. I clicked on the television and turned the volume to loud.

By the time Momma Dolly, carrying a large bakery box, came through the front door, I was curled up on the couch encouraging my inner Amazon to show up so I could tell my grandmother she couldn't stay here any longer.

"The kitchen sparkles, Agatha." She put the bakery box on the counter

I got up, took the salad from the refrigerator and asked her to explain the new bedroom arrangement.

"I forgot to mention to you that I spoke to Mr. Dent two days ago. He refused to back down." She sniffed and closed her eyes for a moment. "He told me I was welcome to keep Miss Priss. He was getting a tom cat from the local shelter."

Momma Dolly burst into tears. I wrapped my arms around her and drew her close. "You're welcome to stay with me as long as you want. And Miss Priss too."

Momma Dolly wiped her cheeks and sniffled. "Thank you, Agatha. Do you mind so much that I replaced your bed?"

"No. It will be nice to sleep in a bed again."

"Your double bed is in our new storage space. Harold said he'd be happy to remove the twin beds and return the double bed if that's what you want. But I couldn't stay here another night if it meant you had to continue sleeping on the couch and Mrs. Simmons . . ."

". . . had twin beds and an armoire for sale?"

"Yes."

We sat down to eat.

Momma Dolly took her time looking over the pizza before choosing the slice with the most pepperoni.

"How many hours a week will you be working?" I asked.

"Not many. Gerda's delighted to have someone willing to fill in for her on occasion. She said Hans hates dealing with the public and would grumble for days whenever she asked him to take over for her."

"Amazing how things work out."

"It is, Agatha. I feel I was fated to end up here."

And my fate is to end up where? I had to wonder if I'd taken a wrong turn.

Momma Dolly, Miss Priss and I curled up on the couch to watch this week's calamity at Crane's Corner on the television. It was clear this show appealed because the small-town setting and the dysfunctional characters reminded me of home.

Momma Dolly's laughter and Miss Priss' contented purrs went a long way toward settling my discontent. By the time I crawled into my new bed, I'd concluded my life was going in the right direction after all, and my self-actualization was taking place in spite of the presence of Momma Dolly.

The next three nights, while I worked at Mitzi's, Momma Dolly sewed new bedcovers and pillow shams for the twin beds on the sewing machine she'd rented from the Rent-All.

On Saturday, I took her to Mitzi's to experience meat-loaf night and to introduce her to Mr. Pritchard, who never failed to show up at the diner on meatloaf night.

Momma Dolly greeted Mr. Pritchard and sat on the stool next to him. I kept an eye on them as I worked. The two were soon leaning close to one another like old friends and conspirators. Would Mr. Pritchard be willing to sign a prenuptial agreement?

Mr. Pritchard got up and went in the direction of the restrooms.

I took the coffeepot over and refilled Momma Dolly's cup.

"Mr. Pritchard's calling a cab and giving me a ride home," Momma Dolly said.

"He's a good prospect for you."

"He's five years older than I am, Agatha, which puts him beyond the good prospect box."

I didn't believe her. She only used her full charm on men she considered good prospects.

A half-hour after Momma Dolly and Mr. Pritchard left, the college kids drifted in. I watched as a group of seven squeezed into a booth in my section. I looked away to check on my other tables. And caught sight of the golden hair and chiseled face of Dirk Koenig coming in the door.

He was back? Had he even left town? What was the point of telling me he'd be gone and then not going or returning long before he said he would?

I took refuge in the kitchen. Mitzi was in front of the

steam table. "You look like you just finished watching a rerun of *City of the Dead,* Aggie."

"Someone I didn't expect to see showed up."

"Your ex-fiancé?"

"No, a man named Dirk Koenig."

"Ah, the devilish and the wicked Mr. Koenig."

"You know him?"

"Sure. He worked as a busboy here when he was in high school."

I could feel my eyebrows rise toward my hairline. So, Dirk hadn't been "hanging out" at Mitzi's to ogle college girls. He'd been working here and ogling them. Why had he failed to mention such a significant detail? I could guess. It didn't fit the new classy image he had of himself.

I re-entered the dining area, my self-confidence high after learning the urbane Dirk Koenig once worked at a job less prestigious than the one I was doing at the moment. Despite his peacock strut and colorful trappings, he started out by working hard and striving for success like me.

Dirk was on a stool at the end of the counter studying the menu.

My knees wobbled.

Courage. You are an intelligent woman with an unlimited future and worthy of respect.

"Hi," I managed to say in a firm voice. "Are you ready to order?"

"A bowl of chili and sweet tea."

I wrote down his order without comment, turned it in, and headed to my other tables to check on customers.

I was not attracted to men with blond hair. I was not attracted to men with egos bigger than Texas.

So, what was it about Dirk that sent shivers running up and down my spine and prickles tap dancing on my heart whenever I got a glimpse of him?

Chapter Nine

Mitzi's was jammed. I didn't have time to stand around and think about my reaction to Dirk. I cleared a booth and took orders from two different tables. When I stopped to take a breath, I noticed Dirk had finished his bowl of chili.

I picked up the empty bowl and refilled his glass with tea. He looked up at me with the heart-wrenching look of someone in serious need of a friend.

"What time do you get off work?"

"Why?"

"I'm offering you a ride home. Compensation for checking on my mother."

"Thanks, but I have another couple of hours before my shift ends."

"Then it's dinner. Any night you're free." He whirled himself around on the counter stool, got up and walked away before I could refuse.

When I got home, Momma Dolly was in bed but wide awake.

She sat up and leaned forward. I reached down to pet Miss Priss who was curled up at the foot of Momma Dolly's bed.

"Agatha, you're not going to believe what I learned about Mr. Pritchard."

I went into the bathroom to get ready for bed. She stood in the doorway.

"What?"

"He has a bowl of wax fruit and a cat that never goes outside."

I laughed with a mouthful of toothpaste.

"Agatha, don't make fun. There's more. And this warmed my heart."

"Okay." I rinsed my mouth and dried my face and hands.

"Mr. Pritchard knew your grandpa and your Great Aunt Tilly. When he was five, he moved to the town where they lived. His family lived in a house one street over."

"So, you and Mr. Pritchard have something in common then? Did he ask to see you again?"

Momma Dolly blushed. I couldn't remember seeing her blush before.

"He invited me to bingo tomorrow night."

I wasn't scheduled to work at Mitzi's tomorrow night but I said nothing. I didn't want Momma Dolly to cancel bingo and deprive me of my first evening alone since she'd showed up. I could use the time to meditate and read parts of my favorite book on getting in touch with your soul.

The next morning, as if by rote, I found myself standing on the sidewalk in front of Koenig's bakeshop. Dirk was back. I'd fulfilled my promise to him. I no longer had to check on Gerda or face the shop's temptations.

I'd say hello to Gerda for the last time and then be on my way. Free of obligation, free of temptation.

I opened the door. Dirk was behind the sale counter. The sleeves of his blue dress shirt were rolled up. The top button of the shirt was undone. A long white apron was tied around his waist. His broad shoulders and leonine head blocked the view of the donuts in the display case.

"Agatha, Hi. Come in, I need to talk to you."

Thinking he wanted to tell me something about his mother, I did as asked, but I stayed near the door and kept my gaze moving around the table area.

"What do you need to talk about?" I asked with one hand on the door.

"About having dinner with me tonight. I checked, so I know you aren't scheduled to work at Mitzi's." He curled his lips together and softened the look in his eyes. "Please."

Holy cow.

The little-boy-lost look on his face and the pleading tone in his voice grabbed my Granny Willa heart. I had to think of a good excuse and fast. "Sorry, but I . . ."

And then Dirk's lawyer eyes skewered me. Waiting for my excuse so he could rebut it.

". . . have to do laundry?" Either Granny Willa, a notorious sucker for a sad story, or my inner Amazon, who'd exposed weaknesses of her own, had undermined my ability to come up with a more imaginative excuse.

"You can do your laundry and go to dinner," he said folding his arms across his chest. "Dinner with me at Groves won't take up more than two hours of your time. I'll pick you up at six-thirty."

Groves was the hottest, newest and most expensive restaurant in town according to the *Millerton Times* restaurant reviewer. My shoulders slumped. My visualization exercise of standing firm if I didn't want to do something for someone else failed—or maybe every part of me wanted to have dinner with Dirk.

Rather than being clear and simple, my goals had become murky and complicated—and confusing.

I was unhappy Momma Dolly was living with me, I was happy Momma Dolly was living with me.

I didn't like Dirk Koenig, I did like Dirk Koenig.

My warring sides had battled to a standstill, but their desire to gain the top spot remained.

"I'll be outside my apartment building so you won't have to park."

He tilted his head to one side and looked as if he wanted to argue the point. But he didn't say anything more, only nodded. I smiled a tentative, unsure-of-myself smile.

On the bus heading home from work at Alldisaster, I considered what one would wear to dinner at an upscale restaurant.

Momma Dolly was occupying the bathroom, getting ready for bingo night. I rifled through my closet.

"If you'd been invited to have dinner at a chi-chi restaurant, which of these outfits would you wear?" I called through the door.

She opened the door. Only one eyelid had been covered with her bright blue eye shadow.

I held the black thrift shop dress in one hand and a pair of dressy black slacks and a sheer black shirt in my other hand.

"Who invited you to dinner?" she asked.

"Gerda's son."

"Dirky?" Momma Dolly turned to stare at me—her penciled on eyebrows had risen to an astonishing height. "Wear the dress."

She turned back to the bathroom mirror.

"When you're finished in there, I need a quick shower," I said.

"Be out in a second. Mr. Pritchard should be here in less than two minutes."

The intercom sounded. Momma Dolly flew out of the bathroom, grabbed her sweater and purse, and opened the front door. "I told him I'd meet him at the elevator," she called over her shoulder. "Have fun tonight, Agatha. And don't worry about the amount of skin the dress shows off."

I shaved my legs for the second time that day, dried off the drippings of shower water and smoothed baby lotion over every inch of my body I could reach. I put on my fanciest set of underclothes and slipped into the black dress. None of my earrings suited. I checked Momma Dolly's jewelry assortment and chose a pair of dangly, black jet earrings. I twisted my ponytail into a neat bun and eased my bare feet into a pair of high-heeled sandals.

Twenty minutes later I walked through the lobby to the front entrance. The sandals, with their three-inch heels, were difficult to balance in. But they were perfect with the dress. The night doorman greeted me and handed me a single blush rose.

"A florist person delivered this and said I was to give it to you when you came out. There aren't any thorns."

I felt my face heat.

Maybe there were no thorns on the rose but there could be invisible strings attached. Before I could tell the doorman to inform the gentleman who arrived to pick me up I wasn't feeling well and would have to cancel our dinner tonight, Dirk's car eased to the curb.

The well-trained doorman rushed to open the passenger door. From inside the car, Dirk lowered the window and handed the doorman a tip.

I got in. The car door closed.

"Hi," I said before I lost my nerve. "The rose is beautiful and a nice surprise. A carnation wrist corsage for senior prom was the last time someone gave me flowers."

Dirk looked to his left to check the oncoming traffic then pulled away from the curb. The soft sounds of a jazz tune filled the interior. He checked his rearview mirror and turned to look at me. His eyes were filled with a tenderness I hadn't noticed before.

"You look great tonight."

I drew in a deep breath. "Thank you, so do you."

"Did you get your laundry done?" he asked. He didn't laugh or smile, but the question lightened the tension.

"No." I laughed and relaxed a bit. Maybe he wasn't the cocky, self-absorbed man I imagined. For a few hours tonight, I would drop my paranoia over Dirk's motives and enjoy myself.

Dirk pulled to the curb in front of Groves. He got out, came around the front, and handed the valet the keys. The valet opened my door. Dirk offered his hand to help me out.

I was grateful for the assistance. Getting in and out of low-slung cars while wearing a skirt requires a practiced grace I'd never needed before. I used my free hand to keep the skirt of my dress from riding up and exposing my thighs that were in need of toning.

The maître d' greeted Dirk by name and escorted us to a table in the center of the room. I took the leather-clad, gold-edged menu he held out to me and opened it to find the writing in French with no English subtitles. No prices were listed.

Across from me, Dirk was "umming" and "hmming" as his eyes moved from the top to the bottom of each page.

A waiter filled our glasses with water. "I'm afraid my French menu skills are in need of a refresher course," I said.

He looked at me over the top of his menu. "Is there anything you don't like?"

"Liver's not a favorite."

"Calf brains, then." Dirk turned his lips into a quirky smile and went back to studying the menu.

I laughed. "Maybe not calf brains." I took a sip. I think my inner Amazon was in charge at the moment. But, never having been in a situation like this, I wasn't sure.

"Diver scallops? Chilean sea bass?"

"Either would be nice."

Dirk engaged the sommelier in a discussion about the wine menu. It was obvious he was no stranger to upscale restaurants or to wine.

With a glass of chardonnay and a plate of four bite-sized assorted appetizers sitting in front of each of us, my education in fine dining got underway.

Dirk picked up his glass and held it toward me. "For service to my family."

I picked up my glass to acknowledge his toast. We sipped and ate.

"Thank you for wanting to compensate me, but my checking on your mother wasn't a burden."

"You deserved a reward for agreeing to do me a favor that forced you to come face-to-face each morning with trays of Koenig's irresistible donuts."

"How do you know Koenig's donuts test my willpower?"

"I believe your grandmother mentioned it." Dirk pursed his lips and then smiled and began to explain what he'd ordered for our dinner.

The waiter refilled our wine glasses.

Dirk began talking about his travels in France and of his experiences with regional French wines and food.

Not in a boastful way, but as one would who was excited over the experience.

I listened with fascination.

And then our entrees were brought.

The food was arranged on the plate like a work of art. I'd never tasted such exquisite food before or enjoyed myself so much—by the time I set my fork down, my plate was as clean as the platter of Jack Sprat and his wife of nursery rhyme fame.

Instead of dropping me at the curb in front of my apartment building, Dirk turned his car into the drive leading to the parking garage.

Sated and mellow from the peaceful ambiance, the good food and the wine, I didn't protest this unexpected maneuver or ask how he knew the entry code.

Instead, I gushed as we rolled into the dim, cavernous space. "Thank you for dinner. The flower was a nice gesture."

He parked and my paranoia struck. Did Dirk know Momma Dolly was at bingo, leaving my apartment free of adult supervision?

I sprung the door handle. "Don't bother getting out. I'll see myself to my apartment."

He ignored me and rushed around the front of the car to meet me as I emerged. He tugged open the basement service door and followed me through the maze of the utilitarian fittings to my apartment door. Now what? What did a handsome, rich, sophisticated man expect from a woman after taking her to dinner?

I kept my back to Dirk and turned the key in the lock.

"Thank you again. Be careful of the pipes on your way back to the parking garage, things poke out at odd angles. One can smack into something before they see it." I turned the door knob, hurried through the opening and slammed the door behind me. I leaned back against the closed door, shaken to the core.

I breathed deep to calm my racing heart and kicked off my shoes and floated toward the bedroom. Dirk's lips were not too fat and not too thin. What would they feel like pressed against mine? Would they be soft or hard, demanding or yielding?

I lay in bed listening for Momma Dolly's return. The hour grew late. I began to worry. What did I know about Mr. Pritchard except that he liked meatloaf, and flirted with all of the single women who came to Mitzi's on meatloaf night? My thoughts took a different and even more disturbing turn. Would Dirk have kissed me, if I'd turned to face him after I'd unlocked my door? And if he'd tried, would I have let him?

I was focused on improving myself—as best I could under difficult circumstances—testing my abilities, seeking a path to fortune, and longing to be the person who talked of their travels. I had plenty to do without including a romantic relationship which would require my paying attention to someone else's wants and needs. As I lay there waiting for Momma Dolly to come home, I devised a set of rules.

Rule number one. No more dinners in expensive restaurants and no more rides in expensive cars until my credit card paid the bill and the car's title was in my name.

Rule number two. Turn tonight's experience into an opportunity to learn French menu and the language of wine to use in the future.

The sound of Momma Dolly in the front room put an end to making up rules. I flicked on the new table lamp between our beds. I sat up and arranged my bedcovers around me as she walked through the bedroom door. I couldn't make a direct accusation of her misbehaving with Mr. Pritchard. I would take a roundabout approach. "How was bingo?"

"Fun. But I didn't win anything. Mr. Pritchard bought five cards for me. Said five cards were plenty for one person. I never play less than ten."

"So Mr. Pritchard isn't such a great date?"

"He paid, but it wasn't a date, Agatha."

She unbuttoned her yellow, neon-green and orange print blouse and slipped out of it. "Mr. Pritchard is keen on a single lady in his apartment building. And she looks the other way whenever he comes by. It breaks his heart. Something else Mr. Pritchard and I have in common is a broken heart."

"Why does he think she ignores him?"

"Because one night he escorted her to meatloaf night but didn't pay for her dinner. She hasn't spoken to him since."

Momma Dolly sat down on the side of my bed and brushed my hair off my forehead. "How was your evening?"

"It wasn't a date, if that's what you're thinking. Dinner was payback for doing Dirk a favor."

"What favor?" She eyed me with suspicion.

"Dirk thought Gerda might be ill and wasn't telling him. He asked me to check on her while he was out of town and then call him if I thought she didn't look right."

"Gerda? Ill?"

"Well no. I don't think she is. But Dirk thinks she's slowed down since he was last home. He was worried."

"What a catch Dirk Koenig would be. He's heir to a profitable business and, with his lawyer's training, he'll always make a good living."

"Dirk is my age, which puts him outside the statistical range to outlive me."

"One must weigh many factors, Agatha. And Dirk's assets far outweigh any liabilities from his advanced age." She shook her head and sighed. "Such eyes he has."

"I'll confide in you. But only if you promise not to try changing my mind."

She patted my hand. "Your secrets are safe with me, Agatha. So, you invited Dirk in for coffee and—?"

"I didn't invite Dirk in."

The expression on her face said she didn't believe me. "Honest."

"Then what do you have to confess?"

I sat up straight. This was important. "I won't marry a man because he can provide a high standard of living. I intend to earn a large enough salary to buy whatever luxuries I desire."

"In that case, Harold is a good choice for marriage. He's young and has a strong back."

"I'll think about it." I laughed along with Momma Dolly.

She stood and moved to her bed.

I snuggled into my favorite sleep position.

"Good night, Agatha. Sleep well. We have a lot of hard work ahead of us."

Chapter Ten

The next morning, it was raining. I stayed beneath the building's canopy that ran from the door to the street and pushed the release knob on my umbrella.

"Watch out for the puddles," Harold said. "People have been known to drown in rain puddles."

Maybe I should marry Harold. He'd keep my inner Amazon front and center. "Be careful, Harold, there once was a doorman who stood out in the rain and melted like the Wicked Witch of the West."

With my umbrella open, I stepped out and lifted it overhead. The gray, lowering sky matched my mood. I should ignore Harold's taunts. Responding encouraged him.

I waited at the bus stop with three others. My nose crinkled. The bus would smell of damp wool and gassy fumes. I considered flagging down a taxi. But even with

Momma Dolly paying part of the rent I couldn't afford to waste money.

I got to Alldisaster and bought a coffee. Its strong odor erased the disagreeable smells on the bus from my nose.

In my cubicle, I found a post-it note stuck on the frame of my computer screen. Mrs. Guilly, the supervisor of the data entry department, said to come to her office as soon as I got in.

At her office I knocked.

"Come in."

Mrs. Guilly, all efficiency and stiff posture, looked up from the papers on the desk in front of her. "Ah, Miss Marple, have a seat. Clever name by the way."

"Thank you." Anxiety over this unexpected meeting had me sitting on the edge of the chair, muscles tensed, like a cheetah watching a herd of antelope.

"Our work load for next week is heavy," Mrs. Guilly said as she drummed a finger on a stack of papers on her desk. "If you're available, I'll have the personnel department ask the temp agency to extend our contract for you."

I wasn't being fired. "I'll be happy to stay on next week."

"Good. Your work is excellent, and you're a pleasant addition to Alldisaster's data entry department."

Basking in the praise, I sat up straighter and relaxed. Could the extension be the advent of my being offered a permanent job? I crossed my fingers.

"Thank you, Mrs. Guilly. I enjoy working here."

Mrs. Guilly waved her hand to dismiss me and turned back to her papers.

My step was lighter as I returned to my cubicle.

When I came out of the Alldisaster Insurance building at five-fifteen the rain had stopped. The setting sun was streaking the sky orange and pink.

Momma Dolly wasn't home when I got back to our apartment. I would call from Mitzi's to check on her. I changed into my waitress uniform and went to catch the bus.

"Agatha, you have the four booths and three tables in the front tonight," the cashier said when I came on the floor. "Dee called in sick twenty minutes ago. I had to re-do the work stations."

I took a mint from the bowl by the cash register. The diner was empty except for a lone coffee drinker at the counter. I went into the kitchen and called home. No one picked up. I went back out to the floor and stationed myself behind the counter next to the coffee urn.

Less than a minute later, my grandmother, wearing a multicolored flounced skirt and a pink ruffled blouse, swirled through the front door. She spotted me and waved.

"Which tables are yours, Ags?" she called out, sounding more excited than usual.

I came around from the counter and pointed out my tables. She claimed the second booth in my section and sat on a bench that faced the rear of the diner. Strange.

"Are you here for dinner? Or because you want to talk to me?"

"I'm combining two things at once, Agatha. You get more done that way." Momma Dolly opened the menu and checked the daily specials. "I hope there's lemon meringue pie tonight."

"I'll save you a piece. Do you want to order now or wait until your party shows up?"

"Good idea. I'll wait, but bring a basket of rolls and a glass of tea."

So she was expecting someone to join her.

I went to fetch the rolls and tea. When I came back to the floor, a recognizable head of blond hair was in the booth with Momma Dolly.

I retreated to the kitchen to wait for the prickles and shivers to subside before I faced Dirk. He wasn't good for me. My Amazon side was susceptible to his charm—not to mention Granny Willa, who got the vapors when he was around.

You always back down, said my nag. *He's such a sweetie,* said Granny Willa. But deep down inside me, my Amazon was holding on. She told me the truth. If you let Dirk Koenig dictate your life and rattle your emotions, you're doomed.

I dragged my feet across the tile floor, set the roll basket and tea on the table, and kept my eyes trained on my grandmother.

"Have you decided what you want?" I asked, keeping my pencil poised.

"Hi Agatha." Dirk's calm voice foiled my attempt to ignore him.

I offered Dirk my waitress smile. "Mr. Koenig, are you having dinner?"

The two conspirators grinned at one another as if they knew the secrets of the universe.

I tried my best to treat them both in the same waitress-friendly way I treated all customers. But my voice sounded stressed and my shoulders had hunched in a protective posture.

I pressed the pencil against the order pad. The lead broke.

I pretended nothing was amiss and pretended to write down Momma Dolly's order before I turned to Dirk—pencil poised.

"A chilidog with coleslaw and extra onions," Dirk said, closing the menu. I wasn't fast enough. His eyes caught mine.

My heart skidded out of control. The fence I had built to protect me from the charms of beguiling men was crumbling. Or maybe the strain of having to deal with Momma Dolly's overabundance of energy on a daily basis had weakened all of my defenses against everything I was trying to avoid.

I delivered their order and kept an eye on them as I dealt with my other customers. It appeared they were engaged in a conversation about a serious matter. The next time I approached their table, their conversation came to an abrupt halt.

When I got home, Momma Dolly was asleep. When I left the next morning for work, she was still asleep—or pretending sleep.

The time had come to have a serious talk with her about her relationship with Dirk and about her going home. I wrote a note reminding her I didn't have to work tonight and looked forward to having dinner with her. I propped the note against the coffeemaker.

I arrived at my assigned cubicle at Alldisaster early. For the second day in a row there was a note stuck on my computer informing me Mrs. Guilly wanted to see me in her office. Hurrah. Alldisaster must have approved her request to have my contract extended.

She confirmed what I'd guessed.

"Miss Marple, I fully expect you will honor your agency's extended contract with Alldisaster and remain with us for the next two weeks."

"Of course, I would."

"Once you've fulfilled your obligation to us, if you're interested, I'd like to recommend you for a job with my brother-in-law. His personal assistant is leaving to get married, and he asked if I knew of someone efficient, practical, and good with detail he could interview. I immediately thought of you."

Me?

Mrs. Guilly uncapped a pen. "As his personal assistant you would be expected to run errands for him, do research for him, and travel with him when he goes out of town."

I lost my composure. Granny Willa tears welled in my eyes. Inside my head, my inner Amazon shouted football game cheers.

"Me?" I said in a high-pitched screech.

"If you aren't interest—"

"I'm ecstatically interested, I think. What does your brother-in-law do?"

"He's Dane Courtney, the mystery writer." Mrs. Guilly beamed at me.

My entire body started to shake as if in an earthquake.

"I know from your personnel file you have a degree in art history. If you take the job, you can make use of your degree."

How?

She handed me a card with a phone number on it. "Call this number for an interview."

For the remainder of the work day, I had to fight to concentrate on my work and to not daydream about exotic locales and wild adventures.

At lunchtime, I phoned my apartment. The answering machine picked up. I didn't leave a message. Instead, I phoned Mrs. Simmons who told me she'd seen my grandmother go out two hours ago but didn't know where. "Try Koenig's, Agatha."

I phoned the bakeshop.

The unmistakable voice of Momma Dolly answered, "Koenig's Bake Shop. Our sticky buns studded with pecans are fresh from the oven. May I save you a dozen?"

My mouth watered at the idea of a warm sticky bun covered with pecans. But the honeyed sales voice of Momma Dolly made me laugh. "So you signed up to push Koenig's donuts."

"Oh. Hi, Agatha. What is it you want? We're pretty busy."

"I called to remind you we're having dinner at the cafeteria tonight." The cafeteria would put Momma Dolly in a relaxed mood—the right mood for her to spill the beans about what she and Dirk were up to.

"I saw your note. Meet me there at five-thirty."

I assured her I would be there and clicked off.

Momma Dolly showed up ten minutes late, smelling like the bake shop and making me hunger for donuts.

"Agatha," Momma Dolly said as we got in the serving line, "I'm sorry I was late. Dirk hired two high school girls to pass out coupons for a free Koenig's donut. We had a rush of customers from three-thirty until closing."

I must have looked shocked because she patted my arm and made cooing sounds the way she did whenever I was confused or overset. Come to think of it, she'd treated Dirk in the same manner the night we'd found him at the diner nursing his feelings over the delivery of his divorce papers.

I picked up a plastic tray and a bundle of utensils. "How many hours are you scheduled to work this week?" I asked as I eyed the salads.

"Free donut coupons will be passed out to the lunch crowds tomorrow. I'll be working from twelve till six. For a couple of hours in the morning, I'll be working as a part-time consultant."

I took a bowl of tossed salad and asked for the low-cal dressing. Momma Dolly chose my favorite, the carrot salad, and added a dish of macaroni salad. She chose a fried veal cutlet that sat atop a mound of spaghetti with tomato sauce.

I ordered the roast beef. I was stunned. What could she be consulting about? She'd never worked in, much less owned, a bakery. She'd worked as a secretary at a public relations firm for a number of years and then for a theatrical agent whose clients were second-tier actors and actresses. Koenig's had been well-established for years. And, as far as I could tell, they had plenty of regular customers to keep them in business. I put a slice of pecan pie on my tray.

At our table I let her eat for a few minutes and then tried to come around to my real question from the side. "Where will you be tomorrow morning, in case I need to reach you?

"You sound edgy, Agatha. Your blood sugar must be low. Eat some of my cornbread."

I ate a small piece of her cornbread and half of my dinner before I mentioned my pending job interview. When I did, and said I'd have to travel, Momma Dolly's face fell.

"We're having such fun, Agatha. Two single girls on the town. Why would you want to be away?"

I choked on a piece of lettuce. "Are you staying in Millerton forever?"

"I haven't made a final decision but I'm pretty close." Momma Dolly's voice wavered. She put down her fork and dabbed at her eyes with her napkin. "I thought, by now, Mr. Dent would have called, begged me to come back, and agreed to sign the prenuptial agreement. But he hasn't called once to say he misses me, and I can't go home until he does."

I changed the subject. I didn't want to talk about Mr. Dent's stubbornness or what it implied.

"Tell me about your consulting work? Who are your clients?"

"Dirk. He's thinking of buying the building next door and using the bottom floor to add a grill to the bakery.

They'd have a full breakfast and lunch menu. He's also considering the idea of opening a branch store on the other side of town. If these are a success, he may franchise. I've been encouraging him and helping him clarify his thinking."

And loaning him money?

Momma Dolly was the last person anyone with a tad of common sense would ask to help them clarify their thinking. I had to believe there was an ulterior motive in drawing her into this scheme. Dirk could be using his charm to open up Momma Dolly's bank account like her second husband.

"And his parents agree to him taking over their business?"

"I think he's encountered a bit of hesitation. He said they're not persuaded taking such a big risk is a good idea."

"So Dirk hired you to help change their minds?"

"Only to make positive comments about the idea— if I'm asked for my opinion."

"Is the free donut coupon part of Dirk's scheme to expand the business?"

"Great idea isn't it? I suggested it. And Dirk did the market research. The results have been even better than we expected. In the last five years, two twelve-story office buildings and a medical complex have been built within walking distance of the bakeshop. A big crowd spills out of those buildings Monday through Friday between twelve and two."

"I suppose Dirk calculated the cost of giving away free donuts and then made an educated prediction of the increase in revenue from the resulting increase in sales."

"He has a good head on his shoulders, Agatha."

I pondered the cost of producing the average donut. My dormant anxiety over Momma Dolly's schemes slithered out of its cage. Alarm bells ricocheted around my brain.

"So who's financing Koenig's promotional giveaway?"

Momma Dolly pointed at my dessert. "Are you going to finish your pie?" The tines of Momma Dolly's fork were poised above the remainder of my pecan pie.

"No." My stomach had taken the brunt of my anxiety and couldn't handle anything more to digest. I handed my plate to Momma Dolly. She scraped the plate with her fork as thoroughly as I'd cleaned off the donut plate with my finger on the day I began my transformation.

I got up to refill my coffee cup and Momma Dolly's tea. I wasn't finished with my questions. I sent out a plea for my Amazon to show up and help.

When I returned to our table, I gave up on finesse and blurted out my real question.

"What were you doing with Dirk at Mitzi's last night?"

She looked surprised. "It was Dirk's suggestion to meet there."

"When I'm working at Mitzi's, please meet with him somewhere else. I don't appreciate Mr. Koenig showing off when I'm trying to earn an honest living. It throws me off stride."

"Who are you talking about? Dirk?"

"That is precisely who I'm talking about." Heads turned. My raised voice was too loud for a public space. I clenched my teeth and lowered the volume to a stage whisper. "Dirk offered to pay me to check on his mother. When I refused to take his money, he invited me to dinner and took me to a restaurant so upscale the menu was in French and no prices were listed. And then, last night he left me a five-dollar tip. The bill came to eleven dollars and thirty-six cents. I plan to give him back three of his tip dollars."

This wasn't the direction I meant for the conversation to go. I wanted to know if Momma Dolly was bankrolling the free donut giveaway or investing her money in Dirk's planned expansion. It made sense that Dirk's money was dwindling. He no longer had an outside paying job, his divorce had likely been a drain on his assets, and I doubted he'd want to risk whatever remaining money he had.

Momma Dolly patted my hand without speaking for a few seconds and looked at me with sad eyes.

"I think Dirk likes you, Agatha."

"Fine. I don't like him."

"Okay. There's no reason you have to like him."

"Thanks."

"But I wish you'd reconsider."

"I've tried to be pleasant to Dirk. But he flaunts the fact he has, or once had, tons of money, and sometimes his manner toward me is condescending."

"Maybe he's trying to impress you because he likes you."

"Tell him to stop."

Momma Dolly patted my hand again. "Give him back two dollars instead of three. You earned the extra dollar."

Chapter Eleven

Even though I still hadn't learned if Momma Dolly was investing in Dirk's expansion scam, our conversation at the cafeteria must have been cathartic. When I left the apartment for the library on Saturday morning, I felt both physically and spiritually lighter than I had in weeks.

Before I went out, Momma Dolly handed me one of the free Koenig's donut coupons.

I would not be going within a mile of the Koenig's bakery again. Not only did they have tempting donuts, they had a tempting son. And walking the extra blocks to the library would earn me my exercise star for today.

I gave the coupon to Harold.

So far, my healthful living chart was pretty spotty when it came to stars. There was the one I'd awarded myself on my first exercise day and then a couple more for days when I'd managed to keep to my healthy eating plan, but with Momma Dolly having taken over my world, my vow to change my bad habits into good habits became even more difficult.

One saving possibility remained—a thin thread of hope for the future—the job interview with Mr. Courtney. Like a pitching machine, the universe tossed me an opportunity for what could be the job of my dreams.

I skipped up the steps to the library, tossing words of thanks into the breeze. I was looking for books on French cooking and on wine to begin my education in fine dining. The dinner at Groves had expanded my universe when it came to eating. And one day, when I had my own office on the executive floor of a large company, I would invite people to dine with me in upscale restaurants and pay the bill on my corporate credit card. Or, at the very least, if I dined in a gourmet restaurant again, I would understand the menu and be able to offer comments about the wine.

I checked with the reference librarian, who pointed me toward the six hundred section. I ran my eyes over the titles of the cookbooks and pulled two gourmet French cookbooks off the shelf. I thumbed through. Jambon translated to ham. Jambon would go into my "to order" column. Foie translated to liver. Foie would go in my "never order" column. I found a book on wine that looked simple enough to understand. I checked out all three books and decided to get a coffee at the nearby gourmet coffee shop, sit in the park and begin my education in fine dining.

I stood on the library's entrance terrace and breathed

in a good amount of the scent of spring—a time for new beginnings and a time for me to take on a new direction. I crossed my fingers and sent out a long, silent plea to the grantor of wishes department. I wanted the job with Dane Courtney more than I'd ever wanted anything. It wasn't an entry level job in a big corporation, but according to Mrs. Guilly, the art degree I'd worked so hard to earn would come in handy, and I'd have an opportunity to travel.

By some odd coincidence, after I had sent my appeal to the grantor of wishes, Dirk appeared at the bottom of the library steps.

"Agatha. Hi." His right arm was waving like a flag in the wind as he hurried up the steps. His face was wreathed by a huge grin.

I started down and tried to go past him without speaking. He ignored my intentional snub, reached out and took hold of my arm.

"We keep meeting in strange places," he said followed by a forced laugh. "Wait while I pick up a book they have on hold for me and then have coffee with me."

I pondered his request for a second or two. Maybe, if I faked friendliness, I could find out if he was scamming Momma Dolly. It wasn't difficult to believe Dirk had the heart and mind of a swindler. And I had to find out. If Courtney offered me the job, I couldn't accept until I knew my grandmother wasn't being conned into investing her money in Dirk's shady schemes.

Granny Willa had taken charge, reminding me it was my duty to save Momma Dolly from her inability to be skeptical about peoples' motives. From the time I could reason, I'd been her voice of caution, and old habits are hard to shake.

"Okay," I said with a smile. "But, I can't stay long."

"Great, I'll be right back."

While I waited for Dirk, I skimmed through one of the cookbooks. My mind wandered off to wonder what kind of man Courtney was. Would he have expensive and sophisticated tastes like Dirk? His books hit the best-seller lists, often sitting at number one for several weeks. He must earn enough to afford whatever he wanted. Did he travel in a private jet? Did he stay at five-star hotels and dine in restaurants reserved for the rich and powerful?

I looked down at the open page of the cookbook. "Fromage." I said the word out loud, but I had no idea if I was saying it right. If I'd known the menus in chic restaurants were in French and that one day I would be invited to dine in one, I would have signed up for French class in high school instead of Spanish.

The library door flew open. Dirk rushed through carrying his book.

"Let's walk," he said. "There's a Bailey's about three blocks from here."

He walked fast, with long strides. A block and a half later I was puffing a bit from trying to keep up.

He turned and looked down at me. "Sorry," he said, slowing his pace. "You don't work out much do you?"

I breathed in a large amount of air through my nose and let it out through my mouth in a loud swoosh. "No."

I wanted to turn around and leave—let him go on his

way without me. But trying to find out if Momma Dolly was in over her head was more important than standing up for myself at this time. If I asked Momma Dolly, she would not tell me. Dirk was my only source.

Seated at an outside table with a plain coffee, no cream, no sugar, I stowed my library books underneath the table. He laid his book on the table in plain view. I looked at the title, *Franchising Your Business.*

I smiled and gestured at the book. "You aren't planning to franchise Koenig's are you? Bakeries are a dime a dozen around the country." I managed to keep a neutral tone in my voice.

"Why are you being hostile, Agatha? I'm exploring the possibilities. Is there something wrong with wanting to grow a successful business?"

"Sorry." I broadened my smile. "I'm under pressure."

"If you joined a gym and toned up, maybe you could handle things without getting stressed."

My tolerance of Dirk's overbearing personality was used up. The bricks in the fence surrounding my heart that had started to crumble were reset and cemented in place.

"And maybe if you were not such an overbearing know-it-all Dirk, you'd have friends."

I reached down to pick up my books.

He took hold of my arm. "Aggie, I'm sorry. Really sorry. I've been trying to climb down from my sanctimonious perch." He grinned. "The fact my parents think I'm perfect doesn't help." He sobered than narrowed his eyes and somehow forced me to look at him. "Confessions of my heart. You are the first person I've cared enough about to try to change. Not only do I think you are beautiful on the outside, I think your soul is beautiful."

He let go of my arm. I wrenched my eyes away and retrieved my books. I steeled my spine, stood, and left Mr. Koenig sitting alone with his latte and my untouched cup of calorie-free, decaf coffee. Dirk could charm a snake. Charming Momma Dolly into giving him whatever he wanted would be easy for him, but the Amazon side of me was immune, vaccinated against the allure of charming men by Jake the louse.

I took the short route home. I waved at Gerda through the bakeshop window as I hurried past. Did the Koenigs have a clue about how insufferable their son was? I decided to stop and suggest to Gerda they refuse to go along with Dirk's expansion plans. I turned around and went in.

"Chicky, I'm glad you stopped. I've missed you."

I reached out and patted her hand. "And I've missed you, Gerda. I stopped to thank you for hiring Momma Dolly for a part–time job. It's what she needed to keep busy."

"I know. So sad about Mr. Dent. All those years wasted."

I eyed the cakes in the glass case. "I understand Dirk has been making plans to expand your business."

Gerda pursed her lips and narrowed her eyes. "Hans hired another baker, part-time. The free donut coupon caused such a rush Hans couldn't keep up."

"Once you taste a Koenig's donut, you can't forget them," I said as my eyes strayed to the display case behind her. "I hope you gained a number of new customers from the promotion."

"Every day. Yesterday we sold out of our frosted donuts before eight."

"So you're planning to open a second store?"

"Maybe we'll put in a grill for breakfast and lunch. Dirky says he'll stay and work here so Hans and I can retire whenever we want."

"So much extra work and worry," I tossed in. "With an expansion of the business, how would Dirk manage it on his own?"

Gerda frowned. "We'll see. Once our boys got their education, they didn't want to make donuts. Maybe, when Dirky gets over his divorce, he won't want to again."

So Gerda and Hans were being cautious. Good.

I patted Gerda's hand and made my good-byes.

I entered the apartment building lobby. Mrs. Simmons was behind the desk. Perhaps she knew something about what Momma Dolly was planning. I walked over.

"Hi, Mrs. Simmons, I don't suppose you know what my grandmother is up to?"

"She's out looking for furniture," Mrs. Simmons said and then her face paled. She pressed a finger to her lips. "I'm not sure I was supposed to tell you."

"Thanks. I won't mention that you told me where she went."

"I'm sure you worry about her, Miss Marple. At Dolly's age, my grandmother took to wandering. We spent hours searching for her."

"I do worry." I began to hum "Somewhere Over the

Rainbow" to block out thoughts of Momma Dolly wandering off. And then Mrs. Simmons' words struck me like the snap of static electricity.

Furniture?

Why was Momma Dolly out shopping for furniture? I sagged. I had no reservoir of energy left to worry anymore about anyone or anything. Sooner or later I'd find out why. And no amount of worry would change a thing.

I got into my pitiful shower and made a decision. I needed to get out of the apartment before Momma Dolly returned. I wasn't in a good enough mental state to hear the reason she went shopping for furniture.

I dressed for work at Mitzi's, and tossed the book I was reading into my backpack. I took the bus to a coffee shop out of the neighborhood, drank soothing herb tea and read until it was time to head to the diner. When I left the coffee shop, the tea and the quiet had restored my emotional balance.

I'd call Dane Courtney's number first thing Monday morning and set up an interview. As chaotic as it was, Momma Dolly had managed her life for years before I was born. There was no reason for me to think I had to save her from herself—or feel guilty if I didn't. If she lost all of her money in a scam, so be it.

I worked my shift and headed home.

The elderly night doorman grinned as soon as he saw me approaching. "Evening, Miss Marple," he said, and made a quick bow—a mature doorman with a pleasant demeanor. Harold should be required to take lessons from this man.

I pushed open the door to my apartment. My lumpy

couch was gone. In its place was a teal-colored sectional. My thirteen–inch television and the rickety table it sat on were gone. In their place was a twenty-five-inch television inserted into a dark wood shelving unit. Tables, table lamps and a red rug completed Momma Dolly's redecorating. It looked nice—colorful—but nice. But it wasn't mine, and I hadn't been asked.

Accepting Momma Dolly's re-do of my space without complaint was something the old "me" would do. My Amazon self would insist on the new furniture being returned and my old stuff brought back—if my lumpy couch, my miniature TV, and my beanbag weren't at the dump.

I filled the teakettle. A folded sheet of writing paper was on the counter.

The inked letters were bold with swirling loops and slanted far to the right. A handwriting expert's dream.

Agatha, sorry you weren't home when I got back. I went ahead and had the new things brought in. If you don't like them, we can send everything back on Monday. Your old stuff is in the new storage area. Don't wait up, I won't be home until late tomorrow morning.

I took off my work clothes, tossed them in the dirty clothes hamper, and put on my robe. The quiet was a bit disconcerting. I poured tea, found the novel I'd started reading before my grandmother had moved in, and settled down. I had the rest of the night and part of tomorrow to myself. I would not waste my anticipated respite.

But I couldn't relax.

The longer Momma Dolly stayed, the more complicated my life became. I'd tell her she had to go, but the new "me" wasn't strong enough. And if I tried to explain her chaotic lifestyle created stress for me, she wouldn't believe me.

I thought about calling Mr. Dent in the morning. I would beg him to call and ask her to come home—but I changed my mind. If I inserted myself into the middle of her relationship with Mr. Dent, I'd be doing the same thing Momma Dolly did to me.

I'd accept the new furniture, say nothing about her leaving, and pray Dane Courtney hired me. Traveling with him would provide the opportunity to breathe again.

I opened the refrigerator and eyed the contents. I broke off a piece of cheddar cheese and popped it into my mouth.

Even though it was late, my mother would still be awake. Her working hours, when she had a role in a stage play, were from late afternoon to early morning. She kept to that schedule even when she wasn't working.

I dialed her number.

"I'm sorry but no one is—"

"Mom? Hello." A touch of panic in my voice made me sound as desperate as I felt.

"Oh, hi Agatha. How are you? And how's Dolly?"

"We're both fine. I called to ask if you'd spoken to Mr. Dent recently."

"Yesterday. At Stimson's Hardware. He was buying a new cat door. Said the one he'd installed for his old cat was too small for the new tomcat."

"Did he say anything about Momma Dolly?"

"Not a word."

"Would you ask him to call her? You know I love her more than coffee ice cream, but she's driving me batty. She's gotten involved in the lives of all of my acquaintances here, and today, without telling me, she redecorated my apartment."

"I know dear. I'll see what I can do to help in a couple of weeks."

I thought I heard an undertone of relief beneath my mother's commiseration.

"By the way, I have a job interview with Dane Courtney, the mystery author."

"Really?"

"As his personal assistant. If he hires me, I'll have to travel, and Momma Dolly will be left here on her own when I'm away."

"Don't be too hasty about taking the job, Agatha. Check out the man's background. Talk to the police chief. A young single woman from a small town traveling alone with a sophisticated man of the world could be a lethal combination if one wishes to protect her virtue."

She must have been reciting the plot of a play she'd been in or a movie she'd seen. Protecting my virtue had never come up before.

Besides, Dirk Koenig was already testing my virtue . . . the virtue that kept me from committing murder.

"Mom, Dane Courtney is Mrs. Guilly's brother-in-law. She was my supervisor at Alldisaster. I don't think she'd recommend me for a job with someone who has a criminal background."

"Okay. I'm writing this down so I'll know who to contact when you come up missing. How do you spell the name?"

I spelled out Guilly and gave her the number of Alldisaster's data entry department.

"Let me know the result of your interview, Agatha. Night." She broke the connection.

I could tell my mother was happy to have me dealing with Momma Dolly. With the same high-energy, illogical personality, and stubbornness, they butted heads over almost everything. And my getting caught in the middle of their spats had played a large part in my taking on the persona of Granny Willa as mediator.

Momma Dolly singing along with the radio woke me. The clock showed quarter to seven. I untangled myself from my twisted bed covers and staggered to the doorway between the bedroom and the living area.

"Momma Dolly, you're back early."

"My plans changed. I've got a busy day ahead of me," she replied and cracked an egg.

"Doing?"

"I'm meeting Mrs. Delman and Mr. Pritchard at their church. After the service, there's a potluck social to welcome the new pastor. I'm making my macaroni and cheese casserole to take. They asked me to invite you."

"Thanks, but I have a lot to do today myself."

"Could you do me a favor, Agatha?"

"I don't know."

"By the way, how do you like the new furniture? I think it warms up the room."

"It looks nice. What's the favor?"

"I called Gerda this morning. She saved one of her chocolate cakes for me to take to the potluck. The bakery is donating it as a good way to advertise. I told her I'd be there to pick it up at quarter after seven before she leaves for church. But I sat down with a cup of coffee and got to talking and I'm running late."

"You want me to pick up the cake for you?"

"Let me call to see if Gerda's still there."

Momma Dolly got hold of Gerda and told her I was on my way in five minutes.

I brushed my teeth, splashed water on my face, and slipped into a pair of jeans and a knit shirt and headed off.

Gerda, dressed in her church clothes, was waiting. As soon as she saw me, she came to the door and handed me a cake box. "Good Sunday, Agatha."

"Thanks. Good Sunday to you, Gerda," I said and reversed course.

I neared the cross street.

And spotted Dirk on the opposite corner dressed in workout clothes. "Hey, Agatha. Wait up."

If I wanted to stop running into Dirk everywhere I went, I needed to move out of the neighborhood and stop working at Mitzi's. If I got the job with Mr. Courtney, I would give notice at Mitzi's and search for an apartment in another neighborhood.

Why did Dirk treat me like an old friend anyway? My silent and abrupt leave-taking yesterday would have discouraged most people. I waved in a motion meant to shoo him away and started moving as fast as I could. The large cake box threw me off a measured stride. Unburdened, and with his longer legs and better physical condition, he caught up to me in no time. He lowered his arm in front of me like a railroad crossing guard. Dirk had some of the same characteristics as my grandmother.

I attempted to intimidate him with a fierce glare. "I don't have anything to say to you," I said with my teeth bared.

His warm smile melted my heart.

He looked contrite. "I'm sorry for being such a jerk yesterday. If you accept my apology, I promise to work harder on not being a jerk."

He twisted each feature of his handsome face into an odd shape. I laughed without meaning to.

"Can we call a truce and start again?" he asked.

Dirk would be a great actor if he wanted to pursue a career on the stage. His eyes pleaded, his lips curled in, his head bowed, like a person who wished absolution. My inner Amazon wrestled Granny Willa and emerged victorious allowing me to overcome my innate desire to try to heal everyone's internal wounds.

"You grew up in this town, Dirk. You must have friends here you could talk to?" My Amazon side was on the battlefield. I gave myself three cheers.

The sorrowful expression remained on his face. "Baggage, Agatha. A lot of baggage full of perceived notions and old hurt comes with old friends."

"And you think I could be a friend without any baggage?"

"I've watched you treat my mother and your grandmother with respect and consideration. I think despite your attempt to conceal it, you have a compassionate nature. And I never feel the need to hide my real self when I'm with you."

"But I do have baggage, Dirk. It's hard to forgive your being rude and condescending."

The neighborhood homeless guy shot us a look as he rolled his overloaded grocery cart around us.

Dirk looked down at the sidewalk. "You're not the first person to tell me this. But you're the first person I've said this to. Being rude and condescending is my defense." He looked up at me with soulful eyes.

In the minute it took me to think about this, Granny Willa charged to the front of the line.

"So, okay then. I'm willing to try being friends with you. But if it doesn't work out, neither of us holds a grudge. We just get on with our lives and pretend we never met."

I started walking toward my apartment building.

He kept in step beside me. "Then say you'll go to the beach with me today. I know a special place where we can sit and watch the waves smash against the rocks. I'll bring lunch. The combination of salt air and sunlight is magical."

I hadn't been to the beach since I was twelve. Today's sweet morning air promised a perfect beach day. I was tempted to say yes, but trying to resist. By the time we got to the front of my apartment building, I'd talked myself out of all reasons I could think of to refuse.

"I'd love to."

"Great. I'll pick you up in an hour."

Excitement mixed with apprehension twirled through

my tummy. But something had alarmed my nag. Why didn't Dirk have friends here that he could go places with? He grew up here. Why did he keep trying to make me his friend?

Maybe I'd find out today.

Momma Dolly was putting her casserole dish into the oven.

I set the cake box on the dining table. "Have fun today," I said. "I don't know what time I'll be back."

"Okay."

I got a break. She didn't ask where I was going or what I'd be doing. Which was great. If she knew I was going to the beach with Dirk, she'd assume things about our relationship that weren't true.

He picked me up on time. We didn't talk much on the two-hour drive, and when we did it was about the weather or some other neutral subject. The rest of the time, the music playing on his CD player created an easy and mellow mood.

The parking lot bordered a steep decline to a small beach area. The moment I got out of the car, I breathed in the briny scent of the ocean and listened to the rhythm of the waves. Every side of me melded into this natural environment as if being by the ocean was where I belonged.

Dirk handed me one of the two small collapsible coolers he'd brought. He grabbed two rolled-up straw mats from the back of the car and tucked them under his arm. I followed as he led the way down the cliff toward a secluded cove.

"My secret spot," he said as he held out his hand to help me leap from a ledge that jutted out over the sand. The crashing of the waves as they hit the rocks, the kiss of a light breeze coming off the ocean, and the touch of warmth from the sun created the most relaxing surroundings I'd experienced in a long time.

I was happy I'd agreed to come. It was beautiful; the perfect setting for an introverted water child to recharge her energy.

Dirk unrolled the mats, placing them side by side. The two collapsible coolers sat between us—a welcome barrier. He took a slim book from the front pocket of one of the bags and opened it to a dog-eared page.

"Wordsworth. Shall I read aloud?"

"Please." No man had ever read poetry to me before. I'd always imagined it would be a strange experience, but with Dirk it didn't seem odd or effete. I leaned back on my elbows and closed my eyes.

"Nutting. My favorite of Wordsworth poems," he said.

He read with the ease of a person reading familiar material. His deep, undulating voice floated above the sound of the crashing waves. I kept my eyes closed and opened my soul to experience the fullness of this time and this place and this man beside me.

". . . one of those heavenly days that cannot die . . ."

I concentrated on the words as he read. What did this poem reveal about this complicated, intelligent and successful man?

". . . In gentleness of heart; with gentle hand touch, for there is a spirit in the woods."

Every warring side of me merged, captivated by the beauty of the words and of the beauty enveloping us.

Dirk closed the book and gazed out at the ocean. He didn't speak again for a long time.

I listened to the shore birds caw, watched the waves, and filtered beach sand through my fingers. Next payday, I would buy a copy of Wordsworth's poems.

Dirk pulled his knees to his chest and locked his arms around them. He rocked back and forth.

I curled myself into a similar shape and waited for him to break the silence.

He looked at me for a second and returned to staring at the ocean.

"Beautiful isn't it. And powerful," he said with a haunting softness in his voice.

"Hmmm," I responded.

He touched my arm and pointed to the dark clouds moving our way. "And ominous," he said. "Those clouds intend to shower us with rain and dance lightning around our feet." He chuckled.

Still, we didn't leave. We sat a while longer as the breeze picked up, the waves grew, and the rain clouds moved closer.

Thunder rumbled in the distance. A drop of rain landed on my nose.

"We'd better go," Dirk said getting to his feet.

We rolled the mats. I carried the lunch coolers. Dirk carried the mats. We clambered up the rocky hill as fast as we could—racing the storm.

Thunder rattled the heavens. A burst of light flashed on the horizon.

Dirk opened the passenger side door. I folded myself inside, dropping the lunch coolers to the floor. Rain drops splattered on the windshield as Dirk ran around the front of the car. He got inside seconds before the rain began falling in earnest.

Sitting inside the car with a CD of classical jazz playing, we watched the waterfall on the windows. Sheltered from the storm, we ate our lunch.

"Thank you," I said to Dirk as I closed the sandwich baggie and plucked a grape off the stem and tossed it into my mouth. I liked this side of Dirk, a side that valued simple things—things that didn't require one to have a lot of money to enjoy. Maybe I liked Dirk too much for my own good.

Dirk wiped his lips with a paper napkin and pulled out a thermos from beneath his seat. "Green jasmine tea. Would you like some?"

"I'd love some." He poured out a cup and held it out to me. I no longer felt intimidated by Dirk's sophisticated air nor threatened by his intelligence. A lot could be said for a man who let it be known he drank green jasmine tea.

"Would you like to talk about your plans for your parents' bakery?"

He laughed. "I was hoping you'd ask. I've spent many sleepless hours trying to decide what I can do, and what I want to do."

"Tell me why you came back home after all of your years away?"

"Hmm." He stared through the windshield. "I was bored by my job, and I was weary of the high-powered world where artifice rules and where besting the other person is everyone's game. Coming home to help my parents seemed like my best chance for finding real happiness—or at least contentment."

"Perhaps we are all lured by the sight of gaudy baubles we think have value."

He looked at me for a long time. I didn't flinch.

"Why did you move to Millerton?" he asked.

"For the same reason you came back. To search for the real me. I love my family, but living with them is exhausting. I get lost in the turmoil that fuels their lives."

"Have you found what you want here? Are you happy?"

"I'm still working on it. Momma Dolly showing up has set back my plan to restart my life, but dealing with her hasn't been as bad as I'd anticipated. With only one family member to deal with I find I can hold my own—most of the time."

Dirk skewed his lips and nodded. "Part of the trick is in knowing what you want and then striving for it without letting yourself get diverted. The hard part is the knowing. By the time we're old enough to choose from all of the possibilities, we've accumulated too many layers to sort through to know what will make us happy."

There was a lot more sensitivity in Dirk than first met the eye. I no longer doubted he protected this sensitivity by being rude. Maybe it wasn't nice but I understood.

The rain eased up. The sun peeked around a cloud. Dirk checked his watch and turned the key in the ignition. "We'd better start back. I promised Pop I'd help him with the baking tonight."

Two hours later, Dirk turned into the drive leading to the underground parking garage of my apartment building. He stopped and punched numbers into the box that lifted the gate across the entrance. He parked in a spot close to the door that opened to the basement.

"Thanks Dirk, for today. It was fun."

"Come on, I'll walk you to your apartment."

"I, ah . . ." In my ears, the beat of my heart was as loud as a marching band's drum line—I could focus on little else.

"No need for you to come with me."

I started for the basement door. Footsteps followed.

I held my breath. I should stop, turn around, and confront him. Defend my rejection of his escort.

He reached around me and turned the door knob. He stood so close his breath warmed my cheek.

Hello. Is there anyone in charge here? Granny Willa? Nag? Amazon?

Silence.

I stepped into the murky basement. Dirk stepped in behind me. "Dirk, I . . ."

"It was nice having someone to share today with," he said in a soft and intimate tone.

"Thanks, I enjoyed seeing the ocean again." I didn't want to state my personal feelings about sharing the day with him. I found my key and turned toward Dirk.

"See you around," I said.

The next thing I knew, Dirk had taken hold of my

shoulders and pulled me closer. I turned my head to one side. His lips pressed my cheek.

He stepped back but didn't let go of my shoulders.

I stared at the cement floor. How easy it would be to let him kiss me for real. With no sense of which side of me was in charge, I lifted my chin and closed my eyes. This time his lips landed on mine. And kissing him felt right.

With a quick breath, he released my shoulders and took two steps back.

I opened my eyes and stared deep into his. Something magical had happened in the salt air and sunlight of the secluded cove. And for this moment, my Amazon side and my Granny Willa side were not sending conflicting messages over what I should do.

Dirk smiled, and his eyes had a dreamy, far away look. And then he reached out and touched a finger to my lips. "Bye, Agatha." He turned and walked away.

The chorus of "Que Sera Sera" reeled through my mind as I watched his retreat.

He didn't look back. The door closed. I could no longer see him.

Whatever will be, will be.

My heart was still wobbling when I pushed the play button on my answering machine. Mr. Dent's voice filled the room. The message was for Momma Dolly. He said his new tomcat was a skilled hunter who came in and went out through the cat door whenever he pleased. She was welcome to keep Miss Priss.

I erased Mr. Dent's message. I didn't want to deal

with a riled up Momma Dolly. And then learned I was too late.

She had left me a note to tell me she was staying over at Mrs. Delman's again. And that, having listened to Herman's heartbreaking message, she was through with him for good. If he called back, and I answered, I was to tell Herman he was a despicable man and not to call her again.

I went up to the lobby to find out the number of our new storage bin and to get a key. I retrieved my neon-yellow beanbag chair and dragged it back to my apartment. I didn't care that it clashed with the new red rug and the teal couch. This was my apartment. I could decorate it however I wanted.

I poured orange juice into a glass, and wiggled my behind into my beanbag and clicked on the television.

Chapter Twelve

The next morning, I got to my cubicle at Alldisaster and phoned Dane Courtney's office. A woman with a well-modulated and pleasant voice answered my call. An interview was scheduled for 5:30. I crossed my fingers.

When you wish upon a star . . .

For the remainder of the morning I concentrated on my work. At noon, I accepted an invitation to join a group of my coworkers for lunch. At five, I shrugged into the jacket of my gray thrift shop pantsuit and headed for the restroom to check my hair and makeup. I refastened my hair, applied a dab of blush to my cheeks and a hint of color to my lips.

The cab I'd hailed took me through a seedy looking part of Millerton then through a working-class residential area and into an area of large homes on large lots.

I looked at my watch to check the time and inquired about how much longer to my destination.

"Couple more blocks, lady."

"Can you pull over?"

I wasn't due for six more minutes. A short walk would help settle my nerves.

"Sure, no problem."

I paid and got out. At precisely 5:30, standing on the entrance porch of a large brick house, I rang the door bell. A woman, whose chic appearance matched the tone of the house, opened the door.

"Agatha Marple. I have a job interview with Mr. Courtney.

"Please come in. I'll see if he's ready to talk with you."

The entrance foyer spilled into a long hall that went through the center of the house to a set of French doors at the rear. I studied the beautiful furnishings from where I stood.

When the woman returned, she motioned for me to follow her. She led me down the hall, through the French doors and across an expanse of lawn to a large studio-type building at the back of the property.

She knocked. A gruff male voice shouted "Enter."

The source the voice was a rather handsome, if somewhat disheveled, man behind an L-shaped desk. The short side of the desk held a computer and a printer. The long side held a jumble of books and papers in messy stacks that looked as though at the lightest touch they'd topple to the floor.

The man wheeled his chair around, tilted his head

and studied me for several moments. I worked at not fidgeting, blushing or turning my gaze to the floor.

"Okay, I'll buzz the house when I need you again," he said to the woman whose name I still didn't know.

He turned to me. "Take the things off that chair and pull it over here," he said gesturing to a wooden kitchen chair in a corner.

I removed the books and magazines stacked on the seat, arranged them in a neat pile on the floor, and pulled the chair closer to his desk.

Dane Courtney appeared to be around forty. He wore jeans and a checked shirt, with the cuffs unbuttoned and rolled to different heights and with the shirttail half exposed.

His eyes kept returning to the computer screen as he asked me questions about my education and why I was interested in the job.

My answers returned nods and pursed lips and more questions. He leaned back in his black leather office chair and began to swivel.

I didn't want my nerves to turn me into a chatterbox like the other members of my family—it wasn't who I was. I answered each question and kept my hands folded in my lap and a smile on my face while I waited for his response.

"So," he said after a pause, "with your background in art history, I could count on you to do a lot of research for me in addition to handling my personal needs?"

"You could."

"Good. And nothing will interfere with your being out of town for a week or two at a time?"

"Nothing." I sat up straighter, glad I wasn't hooked to a lie detector machine. The truth was I was free, but I didn't know if deep down I believed it. I wanted this job with every fiber of my being, but I didn't want to feel guilty about abandoning Momma Dolly.

"Okay, you can start in two weeks. The hours are nine to four, unless I have a book signing or some other public appearance scheduled later. Be prepared to leave town on short notice." He turned back to his computer and began reading the words on the screen aloud to himself.

I got up and made my way outside, pulled out my cell phone and summoned a cab. No one appeared from the main house to take charge of me. I walked down a side yard and waited out front for the cab to arrive. My brain swirled with all sorts of grandiose imaginings. Two weeks to get everything under control—to give Mitzi notice, to finish up at Alldisaster. To get Momma Dolly and Mr. Dent back together.

I called my apartment. Momma Dolly picked up. "Hello." She sounded guarded.

"I'm glad I found you home. Can you meet me for dinner at Mitzi's in about fifteen minutes? I have great news to share."

"Is this about Herman?"

"It's about me."

"You're getting married." She laughed.

"No."

"Okay, I'll meet you as soon as I can. Herman's calling back in two minutes." She hung up.

Was Herman conceding at last? Giving in to her demand that he sign a prenuptial agreement? Begging her to come home? I crossed my fingers. If so, my problem over leaving Momma Dolly was solved.

My universe was circling in a smooth trajectory for a change.

Mitzi's wasn't busy when I got there. I greeted everyone on the floor, and poked my head around the kitchen door to say hello to Mitzi. I settled into a booth with a glass of iced tea. Telling Mitzi I was quitting would be hard. I loved this diner, the people who worked here, and the regular customers like Mr. Pritchard. But I could drop in anytime I was in town.

Twenty minutes later, Momma Dolly came through the front door. Her face looked as if she'd discovered they no longer made her favorite orange hair dye. Knowing she'd talked to Mr. Dent, I was sure her sour expression had something to do with him and that the something wasn't good.

Momma Dolly appeared lethargic as she slid into the seat across from me. She waved her hand through the air in a limp, dismissive gesture before I'd said a word.

But I couldn't stop myself. "So what did . . . ?"

"Don't ask, Agatha."

My heart sank. I studied the menu. "Are you hungry?"

"Not really. My appetite got lost somewhere between agreeing to meet you and the end of my conversation with Mr. Dent."

"Mitzi has lasagna on the menu tonight."

"A cup of soup is all I can manage. But you go ahead."

"The shrimp salad," I said looking up at Annie, our waitress.

Momma Dolly closed the menu and shoved it to the edge of the table. "Maybe I will try the lasagna. If I can't eat much, I can take the rest home."

She looked at Annie. "And bring me a dinner salad with blue cheese dressing." Momma Dolly then sighed.

I watched her move the salt shaker around the table. I kept quiet.

She set the salt shaker back next to the pepper shaker, laced her fingers together, and looked at me.

"After I hung up on Herman, I would have called you back and cancelled tonight, but you sounded so excited I didn't want to disappoint you by phoning my regrets."

"Did I? Sound excited?"

Momma Dolly eyed me with a suspicious look. "You are getting married. Aren't you?"

"Married? To who? Harold?" I laughed.

"Harold could be the right choice for you, at least for the time being. I could be leaving soon, and you'll need a new roommate."

My hand swept across the table knocking off my fork. I couldn't have been more surprised if she'd said she'd won the lottery.

"Leaving? To go where?"

"The fifth floor."

"If you leave, I won't look for a new roommate."

Now I was confused. If I asked questions, I might not get clear answers. I waited for her to explain.

"I'd be happier if you were settled, Agatha. I'd rest easier knowing you had a man to watch over you. After you ran away from home, I lost a lot of sleep worrying about your being alone in a big city."

I cleared my throat. "My news is I've accepted a job offer, and I'll be traveling." I had rushed the words out to forestall her interruption.

Annie set our drinks and a basket of rolls on the table. Momma Dolly spread butter on a roll. She sat the buttered roll on her plate, placed her elbows on the table and leaned toward me. Her eyes were as wide and as unblinking as an owl's. "You sounded so out of breath when you called, I thought someone had proposed to you. I don't see how a job offer could excite you that much."

"The job with Mr. Courtney is the job I've been wishing for." I looked up to meet her doubting eyes. "It's the perfect job for me. I'll do research and travel and put my love of creating order and my penchant for making lists to good use."

"For this writer fellow?"

"Yes."

"Is he a good prospect?"

Momma Dolly's goals for me were centered on the sacrament and sanctity of marriage.

"I met Mr. Courtney for the first time today. He's married."

"And you'll be traveling alone with him?"

"It's a job. If I find he's less than a gentleman, I can quit."

"But Agatha, it isn't proper for a man, a married man at that, to hire a beautiful young woman companion to travel with him. People will talk."

"Not companion, personal assistant. And no one thinks like that today." My loud voice was causing heads to turn again. I leaned across the table and lowered the volume. "These days, men and women work and travel together all the time. This is the kind of job I've dreamed of, and I intend to take it."

"And leave me to rattle about on my own? Fine, Agatha. My entire day today has been ruined by people who fail to accept the truth of my wisdom."

Momma Dolly was breaking her second roll into bite-sized pieces and dabbing them with butter. I reached across the table and patted her arm.

"Tell me about your phone conversation with Mr. Dent."

Momma Dolly finished her salad. Annie set a plate of lasagna in front of her.

"There really is nothing to tell. He called to tell me he's selling his house."

"Why would he call you to tell you he's putting his house up for sale?"

"He said I have a week to move out the things I stored in his basement or he's taking them to the dump. I told him he could hire a moving company tomorrow and send my things here. I also told him he needed to block up his new cat door before his new cat disappeared. He accused me of threatening to steal another of his cats, and if I did, he was reporting me."

"You don't think he was trying to say he misses you and wants you to come home?"

"I'm not backing down, Agatha. When my furniture and my boxes arrive, I'll need more space than our current apartment. So I talked to Mrs. Simmons. There's a two-bedroom sublet available on the fifth floor. Miss Priss and I will be very happy there."

"You've decided to stay in Millerton?"

"I have. And Mr. Dent's name and phone number are erased from my address book and from my mind."

Deep in my center, a sharp pain twisted around and around. A moan threatened to seep through my clenched teeth. I excused myself and headed to the ladies' room. I leaned over the sink and splashed cold water on my face and let the water run over my wrists to cool myself down.

I'd start searching for a studio apartment across town, closer to my employer's house. Mrs. Simmons, Harold, and the Koenigs' could keep Momma Dolly company. And, if I asked him, Dirk might be willing to keep an eye on her and phone me if she didn't look right.

Chapter Thirteen

For some unknown reason, each time I woke during the night and heard Momma Dolly breathing in the bed less than five feet from me, my need for a chocolate-frosted, nut-topped donut escalated.

I hurried my morning routine so I'd have time to get to the bakeshop, buy a chocolate frosted with nuts, and not be late for work at Alldisaster.

I was halfway to the first corner.

"Hey, Agatha." This time the greeting came from behind me. I fought an urge to turn around—and lost the fight.

I saw Dirk's car pulling away and Dirk trotting toward me.

"What's wrong with your car?" I asked when he caught up to me at the corner.

"Why?"

"Your car's going down the street and you're standing here. I thought you had a mechanic come to pick it up."

"Harold—"

"Harold?"

"—is driving my car."

"Why would . . . ?"

"He asked me if he could. And I owed him a favor."

I could not deal with another confusing conversation in less then twenty-four hours. I checked my watch. I needed to hurry or I was going to miss either getting my donut or catching my bus.

"Look, I spent all of last night dreaming about Koenig's donuts. If I don't hurry I can't get to the bake shop and still catch my bus."

"Let's go then," he said, taking my hand and jogging down the sidewalk.

By the time we got to the door, we were laughing and wheezing. Gerda looked up from the tray of donuts she'd been rearranging. She looked startled. "Dirky, Chicky, you're so happy together, so early. So, why?"

Dirk pointed at me. "Chicky, here, needs a donut and she needs it fast or she'll miss her bus, lose her job and not be able to afford to buy our donuts anymore."

"Which donut today, Chicky?" Gerda beamed as she pulled out a pastry takeout sack and shook it open. "Dirky helped with the baking last night."

"Chocolate frosted and—"

"And what are you doing, Dirky?" Gerda asked as she took my donut from the tray.

"I told you yesterday. I intend to bring in more customers and Chicky is my first captive. As soon as she gets her donut, I'll hunt down more innocent people to drag in."

Gerda bagged my donut.

When she handed me the sack with KOENIG'S on it in bold letters, she looked at me without blinking and cocked her head. "You don't come in here so much now, Chicky. Why?"

"You know I'm trying to diet, Gerda."

Gerda sighed—a long, drawn out sigh. "You're too thin, Chicky. It's not good for your face being so thin."

Dirk followed me out the door, laughing. "Instead of taking the bus, I'll give you a ride."

"Thanks but you can't. Harold has your car. Remember? And besides, you have to get on with the business of abducting people and not letting them go until they buy a donut."

"My car should be in front of your apartment building by now." Dirk stepped off the curb, and tilted his head to see. "Yup. Come on," he said stepping back onto the sidewalk. "My coach awaits the donut princess to transport her to her castle. And don't worry, I have all day to wander the sidewalks snaring customers."

He gripped my hand and towed me in the direction of his car. I did not resist or shout banalities despite the fact my nag was yelling at me to save my heart and take the bus.

Harold stood on the sidewalk looking like he'd won the lottery. "Hey, Mr. Koenig. Your car is ultra freaking hot." Harold's grin could have spanned the Mississippi River.

I tossed Harold my donut bag. "Enjoy, Harold," I said in a giddy moment before getting into Dirk's car.

My new ease at overriding the caution signals flashing in my head about Dirk lifted my spirits to stratospheric heights. There is nothing like a sense of danger to make a person feel more alive. And my heart was in real trouble.

Dirk went around to the driver's side and slid in behind the wheel. He stopped the car at the red light at the next corner and turned to look at me. "Agatha, my motives for hailing you this morning weren't pure."

Great! my nag shouted. *You should have heeded my warning.*

"I need to ask you for another favor and thought it would be easier if we were enclosed in a tight space from which you couldn't escape until I unlock the door."

My happy, devil-may-care attitude deflated. Dirk's offer of a ride had been a trap, and I'd fallen in.

"You have a great profile. I love the way your nose curves up."

"Don't you know someone you can ask a favor of besides me?"

"Not for this."

He flashed his teeth, which was a mannerism of his I was tiring of. The corners of his eyes crinkled. "I'm as nervous as I was the first time I asked a girl for a date."

What kind of game was this? Was he trying to flatter me into a stupor? Mesmerize me into doing what he wanted? Dirk had figured out my Granny Willa side and was pushing all of her buttons.

"Thanks for the ride. I'll get out at the corner and walk the rest of the way." How much did I owe this man because his mother had been nice to me?

Zero.

"I need you to say yes, Agatha."

Dirk didn't pull over to let me out at the corner. He found a parking space and parked. I had a good fifteen minutes before I needed to be at my desk. I got out. He got out too.

He hunched his shoulders and hooked two fingers of each hand in the back pockets of his jeans and walked with me toward the entrance of the Alldisaster building.

A few yards before we got to the doorway, he took my elbow and stopped walking. "Agatha, my fifteenth high school reunion is coming up. Will you go with me?"

"What?" I asked, shrugging up the strap of my slipping backpack. He'd asked me to go with him to his high school reunion. I wasn't going to my own high school reunion because Jake would be there. Did he need me to protect him from someone who'd be at the reunion—an old girlfriend, maybe?

He was looking at the people going in the door. "Going to this reunion will be a test for me. It's a test I need to pass if I'm going to stay in Millerton. It'd be easier if I had a friend with me."

He looked at me in that heartrending way he had. We stood on the sidewalk staring at one another while the Alldisaster workers swerved around us. Dirk's eyes, golden in the morning light, were plaintive and pleading. I needed space to make my decision with my head and not with my heart. "I'll meet you for coffee at the donut shop tonight, twenty after five. We can discuss it then." I whirled about and slipped into the revolving door.

On my lunch break, I finished a tuna salad and a pack of saltines and phoned Momma Dolly. She sounded frazzled.

"Are you okay?"

"I'm as tired as a dog chasing his tail."

"You didn't sleep well?"

"Like a mouse in a cage full of cats."

I let out a groan. "So what's wrong?"

"Mr. Dent showed up—two hours ago—in a U-Rent-It moving truck with all of my things packed inside plus a lot of his own things and announced he's moving to Millerton."

"What?"

"I'll explain everything when you get home."

"Okay, but I'll be late. I have an appointment after work. Are you working at the donut shop today?"

"Thank goodness, no. My hands are full with the mess Herman's made."

"Well don't overdo. And don't fret. Nothing has to be settled today."

"Is there a loaded gun in your apartment, Agatha?"

My heart stopped beating. She sounded distraught and serious. I wanted to believe I hadn't heard her question. "I'll tell Mrs. Guilly I have a migraine and come home—right now. Don't do anything until I get there."

"There's no need for you to come home, just tell me where your gun is hidden."

"I don't have a gun, loaded or unloaded, and don't go out and buy one. Why are you asking anyway?"

"I don't want the boys to get hurt by a loaded gun they don't know is there."

"What boys?"

"Harold and his friends."

My teeth clamped together. My jaw muscles clenched.

"Do not let Harold or any of his friends into my apartment," I said as forceful as I could.

"It's too late, Agatha. Harold and a couple of his friends are going to help unload the truck and get my things moved into the sublet. I've invited them here for homemade cookies and milk."

"The lobby"—the words rattled through my teeth like a snake's warning—"serve them a snack in the lobby."

"Well, I never . . ."

"Momma Dolly, for once do as I say and don't argue. I have to hang up. My lunch hour is over." I cut off the connection and tucked the cell phone into the pocket of my backpack. I couldn't dwell on any of this—the unexpected arrival of Mr. Dent, Momma Dolly's moving to a sublet, Dirk's need for a protector at his high school reunion, and Harold being in my apartment.

Dirk was waiting for me outside the building when I left work. "Let's walk," he said. "Not much more than a mile. Twenty minutes, if we walk slow."

Two and a quarter miles. And part of the way was uphill. But not wanting to encourage a remark about my need to get in shape, I didn't protest.

"Sure."

The air was fresh. We passed a pair of mourning doves, waddling about a small patch of grass. Their coos resembled the comfort sounds Momma Dolly made to soothe away my sadness.

Dirk adjusted his stride to my shorter one without making a sarcastic comment about my lack of physical conditioning. He waited until we'd gone a block and a half before speaking again.

"Do you think it's odd I asked you to go with me to my high school reunion where you won't know anyone?"

"Hmm."

"The truth is, Agatha, I have to go to this reunion. It's part of rediscovering the person I was; the part of me that got lost somewhere in the glitz and glitter of a world of power and money. I thought having a neutral friend with me would provide a safe harbor."

There was something in his voice that sounded melancholy. And Granny Willa was a sucker for melancholy.

"Will you go with me?" he asked hunching his shoulders and not looking at me.

The red hand of the walk signal flashed at the corner. Dirk didn't stop. He stepped off the curb.

"Dirk!" My voice sounded loud and commanding like the voice of a mother who sees her child heading into danger. Dirk continued across the street, ignoring me, ignoring the honking horns. He waited for me on the far curb. At some point, thinking he was so distraught he didn't care if he got hit by a car, my heart made its decision. I cared about this man—a lot. I wanted to be there for him.

I crossed on the walk signal.

"Okay. When is the reunion?"

"Saturday."

"What should I wear?"

"You looked great in the dress you wore the night we went to dinner. I think it would be fine. There's dinner with dancing after, but it isn't formal."

"Okay. Good. At least there'll be things to do and we won't be wandering around aimlessly like one does at a cocktail party."

"Right."

We strolled on for a while in silence.

"You seem to have a great deal of free time, Dirk. Don't you think you should find work?"

He turned to look at me and grinned. "A baker gets up in the middle of the night and begins work long before dawn. I've been helping Pops."

I pursed my lips and looked up into his face. "Sorry."

"You didn't have any way of knowing. I'm actually enjoying myself. Every day, you see the positive results of your labor. It's instant gratification for hard work."

We got to the bakery.

"Since the question of going with you is settled, I won't stop for coffee. Momma Dolly is in crisis, and I need to get home."

"Can I help?"

"Thanks, but I doubt anyone can do much to help. Mr. Dent, her long-time friend she refuses to marry until he agrees to sign a prenup, showed up today and declared he's moving to Millerton."

"The rightful owner of Miss Priss?"

"Yes. What time shall I be ready on Saturday?"

"It starts at seven. I'll pick you up at quarter till."

I said good-bye and headed for the war zone.

Chapter Fourteen

Momma Dolly was busy at the stove when I entered my apartment.

"Is that you Agatha?" she asked without turning around.

"It's me."

"As soon as the gravy thickens we can eat."

I stood next to her and draped my arm across her shoulders. She didn't look at me.

"Where's Mr. Dent? It doesn't look as though anything has been moved from here."

"Mr. Dent has installed himself in the sublet and refuses to leave."

"So how are you feeling about all this?"

"I spent all afternoon at a travel agency trying to decide which cruise I was going to take."

"You cannot run away from Mr. Dent again. Talk with Mrs. Simmons. Maybe she'll have an idea of how to handle this. It's possible she can call the police and get Mr. Dent evicted."

"I have my own idea on how to handle this, Agatha, but since I don't want to spend the rest of my life in prison or face the possibility of being strapped into a chair and zapped with high-voltage electricity, I'm restraining myself."

I squeezed her shoulder and made cooing sounds. "After we eat, I'll go upstairs and talk with Mr. Dent. I doubt he's being stubborn just to make you miserable."

"Well if you think that, you don't know Herman at all. He delights in making me miserable."

I sat at the table. Momma Dolly dipped her finger into the gravy, tasted it, and turned off the burner.

"Go wash up, Agatha. I'll dish up the food."

When I returned, my filled plate was on the table, and Momma Dolly was cutting into a large piece of southern fried steak covered with cream gravy.

"So what is it you like about Mr. Dent? He must have some good characteristics?"

Momma Dolly chewed for a while before answering. "Herman makes me laugh."

"And?"

"And he's a challenge. Men usually let me have my way without putting up a fight. Herman stands his ground."

"I've noticed."

An hour later, I was sitting across from Mr. Dent in the living room of the sublet. His new cat, TomTom, wandered about the room in the regal manner of a king surveying his kingdom.

I began my inquiry in a tentative manner. "So, what—"

"Your grandmother is the most intriguing woman I've ever known. I'm lonely and I'm bored without her."

"Then how do you plan to resolve the issue of allowing your cats outside to hunt birds?"

"Don't tell your grandmother, but I took TomTom to the vet. He's been declawed,"—Mr. Dent swallowed hard—"and, ah, neutered." Mr. Dent's face looked pained. "TomTom's not allowed outside."

"And Miss Priss won't be allowed outside either?"

"No."

"Are you really moving to Millerton?"

"I am. At least until your grandmother comes to her senses and goes home with me."

"And then what? Has your house sold?"

"My house isn't on the market. I told her I was putting it up for sale, hoping she'd come back to get her things and I could sway her to my side."

Mr. Dent was a purposeful man. I could see why he kept Momma Dolly on her toes. But if he didn't stick to his guns now, he might lose her forever.

Momma Dolly muted the sound of the television when I returned. She looked at me with eyes full of questions. "Did you convince Mr. Dent to vacate my new apartment?"

"He said he's staying forever."

"But, Mrs. Simmons can't let him stay in the sublet. My name is on the lease."

"Talk to her in the morning and have her call the police to evict him."

"Where would he go?"

"Do you care?"

"I'm a compassionate person, Agatha. It would break my heart to toss any person into the street."

"Then you'll have to think of something else. I'm afraid Herman is dug in."

"With his wretched, hulking cat, I suppose."

"His new cat is very handsome. I think TomTom and Miss Priss would get along fine." I covered a yawn. "Bedtime for me. It's been a long day."

"Not half as long as mine, Agatha. I think I'll fix a cup of cocoa to help me sleep."

"Don't stay up late. If you're going to figure out how to get rid of Mr. Dent, you'll need to be well rested."

Chapter Fifteen

By the time Friday rolled around, I had a better picture of Dirk's troubles. He'd confessed he'd grown weary of trying to be the kind of person he didn't like very much. He'd gotten tired of trying to live up to other people's expectations of him. And the woman he'd married, for all the wrong reasons as it turned out, only became more wrong the longer he lived with her. But it had been his wife who had insisted on the divorce.

I'd asked him about lawyers losing their license after being convicted of committing a felony. He'd laughed and assured me he still had his license. I believed him. My big worry over the real reason he'd come back home was gone.

And, to my surprise, Momma Dolly was mellowing.

When I left for work Friday morning, Herman Dent was at the desk in the lobby, leaning on the counter, talking and laughing with Mrs. Simmons. As I exited the building, Harold stepped forward beaming and holding up his left hand to show me a crisp five-dollar bill. "Need a favor Miss Marple? I'm now an entrepreneur with my own business. I'm looking to expand."

"Have business cards made up, Harold."

"Good idea." He mimed holding up a business card. "Harold the doorman, secrets kept, favors discreetly done, works cheap."

"Sounds good."

"Uh huh. So for a small fee, I won't mention to anyone I saw you kissing Mr. Koenig."

I hissed, and rattled the multiple bracelets I'd borrowed from Momma Dolly. I coiled my fingers into a fist ready to strike. "Because, you saw no such thing."

"Five dollars will keep me from saying I did."

I bared my teeth. "Let me dissuade you from earning your living by blackmailing people. The occupants in those buildings, behind the high walls topped with barbed wire and watched over by men with high-powered rifles, are not nice people."

Harold held up his hands in a posture of surrender. "I was kidding, Miss Marple. But I did take a shortcut through the basement the other day and saw two people outside your apartment door."

I glared. I glowered. I advanced toward Harold with the steady and measured step of the walking guy icon. He backed up. His face was a mixture of bewilderment and fear. Harold kept backing up until he was blocked from going any farther by the side of the building. "I give up, Miss Marple."

"Okay. But don't gossip about the tenants of this building if you want to keep your job.

"Your secrets are safe with me, Miss Marple—for free."

What Harold had seen hadn't been a real kiss, maybe a bit more than a kiss between friends, but not much more. And if Momma Dolly got wind of Harold's misconception of what Dirk and I had been doing, she would think my relationship with Dirk was more than friendship. It would disappoint her when she learned the truth.

After work, I got off the bus three stops early. I could use the exercise, even if the exercise was an excuse to go past Koenig's.

A peek through the window informed me Gerda was back in her normal spot behind the counter. I waved. She motioned for me to come in.

I opened the door and stuck my head in. Seeing no one but Gerda I stepped inside and walked toward the sale counter.

"Chicky, I got—"

I shook my head.

"But—"

"Gerda, you know I'm trying not to give in to my weakness for your donuts."

Gerda came around the counter and took my elbow. "Have a seat, I bring you coffee. I have to talk with you."

I visualized myself slapping my forehead out of frustration. Was Gerda going to dump her angst into my ears and my lap too? My plate was full, what with starting my dream job, providing Dirk a safe harbor at his reunion, and dealing with the ongoing problems between Momma Dolly and Herman. My stomach acid churned into a whirlpool. Coffee would only exacerbate it.

Gerda sat two full coffees on the table and dropped herself on the chair across from me.

"You like my Dirky, Agatha?" Gerda's eyes were soft, misty.

I caught my breath. How could I answer her question without saying something that might hurt her feelings or make her think I considered her Dirky a good choice?

"My Dirky likes you."

I cleared my throat and stirred my coffee. "You're lucky to have such a considerate son."

Gerda preened. "You are a good judge."

I felt the tension in my back ease. Gerda had been throwing out bait to catch a compliment about her Dirky.

"Now, what I really have to tell you is Mr. Dent picked up Dolly yesterday. They left, all cozy together. Arm in arm. Laughing. I tell you, because I know you worry."

As soon as Gerda's words sank in, my worries departed about leaving Momma Dolly. Mr. Dent had been forgiven. I would be spared further guilt over leaving Momma Dolly alone when I had to travel.

"Ma?" Dirk poked his head around the kitchen door. His eyes widened. He opened the door all the way and waved. "Agatha. Hi." He hustled into the public area wiping his hands on a white apron around his waist.

"I didn't know you'd be in today. Aren't you working tonight?"

"I am. But your mother tempted me with coffee. I risked being a few minutes late. One more shift at Mitzi's to train the new girl and I'll no longer have to face the madhouse of meatloaf night again." I laughed, but I knew I would miss meatloaf night.

"Sit down Dirky," Gerda said, motioning to my vacated chair.

"Let me see Agatha out first. Be right back," he said. A smile split Gerda's broad face reminding me of the shape of the chocolate-frosted, nut-crusted donut halves that had wrecked the opening day of my transition.

"Such a nice couple," I heard Gerda say as we walked away.

On Saturday night, the intercom in the apartment buzzed. I punched the button. "A Mr. Koenig is here."

"Thanks, I'll be right up."

I found my purse, checked my lipstick, and grabbed the pale turquoise cashmere shawl Momma Dolly had bought for me on one of her trips to the thrift shop.

Dirk was in the lobby, looking out the plate glass window.

I touched his arm. He turned, his eyes were wistful. He was dressed in a tailored black suit, a tie with small figures on a pink background, and a pale gray shirt. He stood still with his hands behind his back looking handsome and vulnerable.

"You look stunning, Agatha."

"Thanks.

"I like your hair twirled around like that."

I think I was blushing. "You look nice too."

My hold on my heart slipped. My thoughts tumbled across my brain faster than a Chinese acrobat. Every inch of me tingled as if I'd touched a live electrical wire. When Gerda said her Dirky liked me, was she telling the truth?

Dirk took my elbow and escorted me out of the building. The sight of a red Ford truck with an extended cab at the curb brought me back to the real world.

"Your chariot, my lady." Dirk bowed, and helped me climb in. Getting into a truck with grace requires different moves than getting into a low slung sports car.

Dirk went around to the driver's side and got in. This wasn't a joke.

"What happened to your car?"

"My fairy godmother showed up, waved her magic wand and this is the result. Do you think she made a mistake?"

I started to giggle.

"You are Cinderella, right?"

"I am."

Somewhere, the birds and mice were singing.

The truck's radio was tuned to a classical music station.

"Your choice of music doesn't fit your fairy godmother's choice of wheels."

"I think she's trying to tell me the contrast between the music and the vehicle is a reflection of the dichotomy of the current me. Selling my car and buying this truck is part of recovering the person who got lost."

I twisted the strap of my purse as I considered this new information.

"Agatha?"

"I'm mulling over everything I thought about you," I said, still not looking at him. "I have a list of words describing you. Most of them aren't complimentary."

"I see."

"There are a couple of nice phrases near the top of the list, like concern for your parents."

"Thanks."

I glanced at him. He didn't look out of place driving a truck while dressed like a mannequin in a high-end men's clothing store.

"Who am I supposed to save you from tonight? Are there names I need to know?"

"Everyone."

Dirk steered the truck into an empty space in the parking lot of Millerton's snootiest country club. He turned in his seat. His face was not smiling. "The truth is, Agatha—"

"Call me Aggie."

"—Aggie, the attendance area for my high school takes in all the upper echelon neighborhoods of Millerton. Most of my classmates have parents who are doctors or lawyers or other high-paid professionals. Some are from the most prominent families in Millerton. On their sixteenth birthday, they all got their own car. During the summers, they traveled to Europe and to family beach cottages. They went skiing over Christmas break. My parents owned a donut shop. I worked in the back after school. The summer of my junior and senior year, I worked at Mitzi's on weekends. I rode the bus."

I took in a deep, shuddering breath. The pain of being

part of a family who was different from the rest of the community was a pain I knew far too well. In my small hometown, Momma Dolly was loved for her big heart. She was always the first to show up with a casserole or iced cake when someone had a tragedy. She volunteered to help out for every good cause. But, by the time I got to high school, I knew her eccentric ways raised eyebrows. And my mother, in the nicest terms, was referred to as exotic. Deep inside, I harbored the emotional pain from being part of a family who didn't quite fit in. I reached out and took Dirk's hand. The common bond between us kindled a flame in my heart.

He looked down at me. His eyes were filled with resignation. "It's okay, Aggie. It's all part of facing the reality of one's life and then being okay with it. Your coming with me tonight helps a lot."

I let go of his hand.

He pulled the keys from the ignition. "Come on, let's go in."

I put my hand on his arm to get his attention before he got out of the truck.

"Every unflattering word I've used to describe you has been erased. You have a clean slate, Mr. Koenig."

"Call me Dirky."

Was he serious? He looked serious, and then I noticed his lips begin to twitch.

"Fine." I giggled. "But only if you call me Chicky."

His finger brushed my lips. His heated eyes warmed mine.

I think I murmured something incriminating.

He got out and came around to help me out.

By the time we entered the lion's den full of his high school classmates my Amazon was in charge and prepared to defend Dirk with every weapon she possessed.

"Dirk Koenig." A tall balding man, with a paunch visible beneath his buttoned suit jacket, slapped Dirk on the shoulder.

Dirk offered the man his hand and turned to me. "Agatha Marple, Jason Hightower." I extended my hand and said hello. Jason's palm was moist.

Jason eyed me in a brazen manner, winked and turned back to Dirk. "Heard you were offered a partnership at Witting, Witting and Witting. Congratulations."

"Thanks, Jason. Nice to see you again."

Dirk dismissed Jason with a quick nod, took my elbow and steered me toward the table number printed on our nametags.

The tables were set for ten. The others at our table were pleasant enough during dinner. Dirk was terse, subdued, answering their questions but not elaborating. I pretty much said nothing, but kept my ears open to what was being said. If I sensed Dirk was feeling insecure, I'd give a reason for leaving the table and request his assistance. Dirk had a heart. He was a sensitive and vulnerable man. He deserved a strong female by his side.

As the night went on, nothing was said that I construed as condescending or sarcastic. In fact, his classmates were complimentary, eager to talk about his success and inquire if he knew so and so or had been to such and such a place. I relaxed a bit and savored the chocolate mousse cake served for dessert.

The band began to play a slow dance tune. Dirk stood, took my hand, and led me to the dance floor. He was a skilled dancer. I followed with ease.

"The wine was terrible," he said as he whirled me around the floor.

"Hmm. Acidic, with no detectable hints of cherry or oak."

He looked down at me. His eyes bubbled with laugher. "So, you've been reading your book on wine."

"I have. One day, I plan to tour the vineyards of France and Napa Valley."

Dirk laughed. "How is your study of French cooking coming along?"

"Jambon is ham," I said with a grin.

He laughed again. "We could drive north next Saturday and have dinner at ZZZ's. You could choose what to order from the menu and the wine list. It would be good practice."

All of a sudden, I got cold feet again. My nag started flashing yellow caution signals about spending more time with Dirk. Mending a broken heart isn't easy. And the scars from the wounds Jake left on my heart were still fresh.

"I'll have to see about Saturday. I'm starting a new job soon, and I have a lot to get done. I'll be traveling. Even though no date was mentioned at my interview, I want to be ready in case it's soon. And there's still a problem of leaving Momma Dolly."

Dirk did not ask me about my new job. Instead he twirled me around several times and drew me back, circled my waist, and pulled me closer than before.

"How are your grandmother and Mr. Dent getting along?"

"They had dinner together at Mitzi's last night. They looked happy."

"A good sign."

"My fingers are crossed."

The music stopped. Dirk squeezed my hand as we started toward our table. As we moved past other couples, Dirk was greeted by several former classmates. A blond, with hair that had the texture of straw, squealed and circled her arms around Dirk's neck.

"Dirk, why didn't you call? I had no idea you were back in town."

Dirk managed to extract himself and keep her at arm's length. "Sally Mandell?"

"Yup. Divorced, and ready to party again."

"Sorry." Dirk maneuvered around her so I got inserted between the two of them. He introduced me, said it was nice to see her again, and took my elbow and hurried me off the floor. We made our polite good-byes to the others at our table.

"Whew," Dirk said as we strolled hand in hand across the parking lot to the red truck.

"Feel better?" I asked.

"Intimidated by them? Can you imagine? What was I thinking when I was sixteen?"

"Probably the same thing most sixteen year olds think about."

He laughed. "You're probably right."

We stopped beside the passenger side door. He pulled me into his arms. My cheek rested next to the side of his head. I stopped breathing, or at least I thought I stopped breathing.

"Ags?" His voice was soft.

"Hmm."

"The first time I saw you, I knew I wanted to get to know you." He gave a soft and gentle laugh. "I think we're a good team."

"Hmm."

One day I'd ask why, but at the moment it wasn't important.

He moved his head back and kissed me, a soft, lingering kiss. None of my warring selves interrupted to spoil the moment.

His lips pressed harder. I didn't resist.

Raucous laughter coming from the other side of the parking lot broke the mood. Dirk opened the door and helped me in.

I pulled the seatbelt across my chest. *You're in deep trouble,* said my nag. *Stay strong,* said my Amazon. The contented purring sound I heard came from Granny Willa.

I snapped the seatbelt in place.

All three of my warring sides had worked as a team tonight, offering up their best traits. My Amazon side had been ready to defend Dirk from any slings or arrows because my Granny Willa side empathized with his pain over being an outsider—and my nag hadn't warned me of trouble ahead because being there for him was the right thing to do.

Dirk drove into the entrance to the parking garage and punched in the numbers that opened the gate.

"Did Harold or Momma Dolly give you the code?"

"Will you have the guilty party charged with treason-ous behavior?"

"I may."

"Then I cannot betray their trust."

"Being trustworthy is an admirable trait," I said and laughed.

"It's a trait I was forced to learn as soon as I could talk. Koenig's donut recipe is a state secret. Being hung by your thumbs is the penalty for revealing it to outsiders."

We were both laughing when he came around to open the passenger door.

This time I did not try to prevent him from walking me to my door.

In the dim basement, standing outside my door, Dirk lowered his face toward mine. He lips touched down— a perfect landing. He tightened his arms around me. Heat and pleasure roiled my emotions. By the time Dirk stepped back his eyes were soft. And I was limp from having lost all of my resistance to this man. He stirred my soul. He needed me. He was smart and kind and funny and right.

Keeping his arms around my waist, Dirk looked deep into my eyes.

I couldn't think. I didn't want to move.

He took a deep breath. "Thanks Agatha. My angst over my teenage years has been vanquished. Perhaps the lives of some of my classmates weren't as wonder-ful as I imagined they were."

"Probably not," I managed to say as I struggled to regain control of myself.

He tucked a strand of my hair behind my ear, and then with the tip of a finger, he traced the rim of my ear. "Night." He turned and started to walk away. I stood there open-mouthed and watched him, marveling at his easy stride. He stopped in the open doorway, turned, and waved.

Once he was out of sight, I recovered enough to get inside my apartment. This was bad timing, a turn of events that knocked me off balance again. How could everything I'd ever longed for show up at the very same time?

I looked in all the rooms. Momma Dolly wasn't home. I checked the clock—10:30. Worrying about Momma Dolly was silly. She'd been widowed three times. She could take care of herself just fine.

I looked around for a note but didn't find one. I could call Mr. Dent and ask if she was there, but then I would be meddling in her affairs, The very thing I didn't want her to do to me. I slipped my dress over my head, hung it in the closet and finished getting ready for bed.

I was in bed reading when I heard Momma Dolly say good night. I put my book aside and sat up.

She came into the bedroom. "Hi Agatha. I'm glad I didn't wake you. How was your date?"

"It wasn't a date. But I had a good time. Were you—"

"Why wasn't it a date?" she asked over the splash of water in the bathroom sink.

"Dirk and I are friends. And that's all. Were you out with Mr. Dent?"

"Hmm. We tried to introduce the cats, but Miss Priss spat and hissed at TomTom. It isn't going to work."

"So the wedding's off again."

"It's possible we'll get married and live apart."

"That could work."

Momma Dolly yawned and climbed under her covers. "Busy day tomorrow, Agatha. I'll wake you in the morning so we can get started."

Now what? Get started on what? It was late. My emotions weren't steady enough for me to think straight. I turned on my side to face the wall and pulled my green blanket over my head.

The smell of bacon frying woke me. I could tell by the faint light filtering through the curtain over the basement window that the sun wasn't all the way past the horizon. I stumbled into the front room rubbing my eyes.

Momma Dolly was dressed for the day, humming and bustling about fixing breakfast.

"It's early."

"Good morning, Agatha. Lots to do today."

"Like?"

"Sit down and I'll pour the coffee."

I got my robe from the closet, tied the tie firmly around my waist, and sat at the table.

Momma Dolly put a platter of crisp bacon and over-easy fried eggs next to a plate holding slices of buttered toast and sat down across from me.

"Okay, Ags. Here's what will be keeping us busy today. This is the best solution Herman and I could come up with for us."

"Who is us?"

"You and me."

I sipped my coffee and closed my eyes. When I opened them, Momma Dolly was still sitting there— I wasn't in the middle of a bad dream.

"You and I are moving to the two-bedroom, two-bath sublet. Mr. Dent is moving down here. TomTom will have the run of the basement, and Miss Priss will reign over a spacious, light–filled apartment. The big window with a ledge in the living room of the sublet is very convenient. She can lounge there and watch the goings on outside."

I shook my head in a negative way. My teeth shattered a slice of crisp bacon.

"What do you think?"

"I wish you'd asked me first. I don't know yet what my salary will be. I don't know if I'll earn enough to cover my share of the rent for the sublet."

"If you don't want to move, I'll cancel everything." She lowered her gaze to her plate and broke a strip of bacon into pieces. She huffed. And then she lifted her chin and looked at me. "I'll cover the rent."

"It would be nice to have separate bedrooms. Maybe my old double bed will fit," I said in my Granny Willa mode.

"And we'll each have our own bathroom," Momma Dolly said. "It's difficult here, cramped. I've had to keep my creams and makeup in a box in my dresser. It's been an inconvenience."

Good grief. She could have gone home, where she had her own bathroom with plenty of storage space. I laughed, but wondered how much longer she'd have been willing to suffer such hardship? I spooned strawberry jam onto a triangle of toast and dipped the end into my runny egg yolk.

"Finish eating, Agatha, the movers will be here at six-thirty. You need to get dressed." She took all the used dishes and utensils to the sink, and filled it with hot water and soap bubbles.

I got up from the table, stretched and yawned.

"You didn't hire Harold and his friends to move us, did you?"

"Certainly not. I hired people who do this work for a living."

At 6:30 the intercom announced the arrival of the moving men. There was a simultaneous rap on the door. I heard Momma Dolly greet Mr. Dent.

When I returned to the living area, Mr. Dent winked at me. A cardboard box sat on the floor.

"For Miss Priss," Mr. Dent said. "She may feel more secure in her box for a while."

"Herman Dent, you are the most thoughtful and sweet-est man I've ever known," Momma Dolly twittered.

A disbelieving sound ruffled the back of my throat. "Where's TomTom?"

"Stashed in a box behind the boiler. He's not happy about moving." Mr. Dent patted Momma Dolly on the head. "You ready to get to work, Dolly?"

Momma Dolly rammed her fists into her waist and gave him her quizzical look. "Work? What sort of work?"

"Movers charge by the hour. If we help, we save money."

Momma Dolly pushed the intercom button. When she got a response, she bellowed, "Mrs. Simmons, send those movers down at once, no sense paying them good money to lollygag about in the lobby."

"Okay, let's get to work," Momma Dolly said and began issuing orders. "Herman, take Miss Priss up to the sublet, and Agatha, start pulling things out of the cupboards. We'll wrap and pack the kitchen things while the movers carry up the furniture."

I got right to work. There wasn't much in my two cupboards and one kitchen drawer. The majority of the set of dishes Momma Dolly bought for me was in a box in our storage bin.

I carried a box of kitchen gadgets up to the sublet. The sun blazed light into the room through the large front window. The kitchen had a window too. And a wall separated the kitchen from the living room. There was a nice-sized dining alcove. Both bedrooms were the same size. Each came with an attached bathroom and a walk-in closet. Living here would be great. I'd have some space of my own again.

Three hours later, everything had been moved from the basement apartment and Mr. Dent's things were moved down.

In the sublet, Mr. Dent was hooking up the television set and Momma Dolly was making chicken salad. I was surveying my new bedroom, trying to decide on the best placement for my old bed that had been rescued from the storage bin.

"Agatha. Do you want a cup of tea? Mr. Dent and I are leaving for church at eleven-thirty. We'll have our lunch when we get back."

"Not now, thanks. I'm taking a shower and then getting some exercise."

I headed for the small park not far from my apartment. The morning air was warm. I sat on a bench. My life was spinning in a hundred new directions, or so it seemed. Momma Dolly was moved in with me forever, I was in love again. I had a new job that promised adventure. But the job would take me away from Dirk. And I had no idea how often I would be out of town or for how long— or even if it mattered to him.

I raised my face to the sun, closed my eyes and tried to convince myself my worries were without merit. If Dirk wanted me to be by his side, riding shotgun twenty-four hours a day, he would have said something by now— maybe.

The battle in my head raged.

You can't have it all, said my nag.

Says who? my Amazon asked.

If you can have it all, you will, said Granny Willa.

The first day of my new job, I knocked on the front door of the Courtneys' house. The chic woman answered the door again. She led me into a room fitted out as a library. She motioned me to a chair and sat down on an adjacent sofa.

"Welcome, Miss Marple. I'm Jan Courtney, Dane's sister and current office assistant." She gave a musical laugh. "The minute Dane heard your name he knew you'd be perfect for the job of his personal assistant."

So he wasn't married to this woman.

She trilled her laugh again and handed me a thin folder. "These are your job instructions. Everything you need to know should be in there. If not, call me. The main thing to remember is you aren't to bother Dane. He'll summon you on the intercom if he wants to talk to you."

I opened the folder and glanced at the first sheet.

"Keep a bag packed for traveling," she said. "I'll be in town for the rest of the week. My cell phone number is attached to the back cover of the folder."

She got to her feet. I followed. In the back of the hall, she took down a ring of keys and handed them to me. "The gold key opens the door to your work space which is in a separate room behind Dane's office. Walk around back to enter. There's an interior door between the two rooms, but unless Dane calls for you, don't go into his office."

My neck muscles tensed. Strange. Maybe this job wasn't my ideal job after all.

"One of the keys is for Dane's car, another opens the door to his half of the office and one opens the back door to this house. He loses his keys on a regular basis. We keep a number of spares in the first drawer in the kitchen."

She got up, motioned me to follow her, and led me out the back door. My feet dragged as we went around to my entrance at the rear of the studio building.

When I saw the room where I'd be working, I felt better. There were two windows, one of them let in the east light, the other let in the north light. The room was spacious with modern equipment and plenty of work area. There were bookcases, a comfy looking sofa and footstool, and a small kitchen area that included a sink. It wasn't the dreary space I'd imagined.

She followed me in. "You're free to bring whatever you like to keep yourself busy if Dane hasn't left a list of things for you to do. He'll leave notes for you in the in box sitting on the table by the door. You can leave notes or research material for him in the out box. He'll pick them up whenever he's ready or he'll buzz you."

She pointed to the bookcases. "I'm sure you'll find a great deal to interest you on those shelves." She gave me a questioning look. "You were told Dane expects his assistant to run personal errands for him on occasion?"

"Yes."

"You can use the Toyota in the garage. The key is on the ring I gave you." She pointed to a door off the kitchen area. "There's a powder room behind the door."

She left. I settled in. The quiet was music to my ears.

On Wednesday, Mr. Courtney came in, said hello, and left. On Thursday, I found a note in my in box informing me we were leaving for Paris on Monday and returning Friday. His sister would fill me in on the details. My heart started pumping as if I'd run a mile. *Paris. Imagine.* I scanned the bookcases and found a section of reference books on France, Paris and the Louvre. There was another book that covered all of the art museums in and around Paris. I curled up on the sofa and began to read.

My cell phone rang. It was Dirk. "Have you decided about going to dinner with me Saturday night at ZZZ's?"

I didn't hesitate. I was going to Paris. The chance to practice my French menu and wine skills couldn't be turned down. And, more than anything, I wanted to spend the time with Dirk.

"Okay, and I have great news. I'm leaving for Paris on Monday and returning on Friday."

"Okay. Saturday. Six-thirty." He disconnected. I was surprised he had ended our conversation without making a comment about my upcoming trip.

When I got home and told Momma Dolly I was going to Paris, she responded by repeating a rule of etiquette from the Victorian age.

"A single woman traveling alone with a man isn't proper, Agatha."

I patted her hand and kept my eyes focused on hers to appear resolute. "I don't think Mr. Courtney will be a problem. But, if I find out he is, I'll quit and buy a return ticket."

On Friday, I came home and found Momma Dolly curled up on the living room couch with a box of tissues in her lap. She dabbed at her cheeks and offered me a watery grin.

Alarm sounds pinged in my head. "What's the matter? Where's Mr. Dent? Was there an accident? Did Mr. Dent back down and you aren't getting married after all?"

Momma Dolly patted the sofa cushion beside her. "Sit down, Agatha. Herman didn't back down or have an accident."

I sat on the very edge, and bent over as though in severe pain.

"Agatha?" Momma Dolly patted my back. "Are you sick?"

"I don't know."

"I'm making tea."

I settled back against the cushions, pulled off my shoes and curled my legs under me. I owed my grandmother for all the years she'd taken care of me. And I couldn't count on my mother or my sister taking care of her. If she needed me, I would be here for her.

She came back with two mugs of tea.

"I'm having second thoughts about marrying again," she said.

"Why?"

"Herman took me to Renael's for dinner tonight. I ordered the fettuccine with chicken."

"It sounds lovely—the kind of evening you enjoy."

"Our food came. I cut a piece of chicken and speared it with my fork. It looked and smelled delicious. I was about to put it in my mouth when Herman looked at me with that strange look he gets in his eyes. He asked me if I knew I was about to eat a dead bird."

A giggle escaped before I sealed my lips to prevent myself from laughing out loud.

Momma Dolly sprang to her feet. "There's nothing funny about this, Agatha. Herman is the most insensitive man I've ever known. And I've known a lot of men in my lifetime." She sniffled and tugged a tissue through the slot of the box. "Why I ever considered him suitable for marriage, I have no idea."

I patted the seat cushion beside me. "Sit."

She collapsed in a heap on the sofa and wailed. "I'm as much of a fool for wrong men as Jade is."

"Did you make a scene in Renael's?"

Momma Dolly looked at me as though questioning my sanity.

"Of course not."

"Okay. So what happened next?"

"I finished my dinner—in silence. Herman insisted on ordering dessert and coffee. While we waited for our dessert, Herman pulled a ring box from his pocket, sprang the lid and presented the box to me. The most beautiful diamond ring was nestled in a black velvet interior."

"And?"

"The waiter set our desserts and coffee in front of us. When he left, I closed the lid and handed it back to Herman. He didn't say a word. He put the box back in his pocket, picked up his fork, and ate his cannoli."

Herman Dent had the calm confidence of a cliff diver. He didn't let Momma Dolly's capricious behavior rattle him. I wished I knew his secret.

"And then you came home and cried?"

"Well, it was a sorrowful realization," she said and sniffed.

"That Herman is a wrong man?"

"Yes. On the other hand, it's good I learned this before I married him."

"Herman has a droll sense of humor, a strong constitution, a steady nerve—and he loves you."

"Do you think he does?"

"If he didn't, would he follow you here, move in, and refuse to go home without you?"

"I'm going to bed, Agatha. I'll see you tomorrow."

A deep weariness settled over me and damped my spirit. I put things away and then got ready for bed.

I lay awake for a long time, staring at the black shapes of the objects in my darkened bedroom. And then in that fuzzy state of consciousness between asleep and awake, I made my decision.

Chapter Sixteen

I was going to Paris.

Regardless of everything going on, I was keeping my new job. I waited for my Amazon and my Granny Willa or my nag to try to discourage me. But not one of them showed up to challenge my decision. For five days, Momma Dolly could handle her self–created troubles without me. And if she was putting her money at risk by investing in Dirk's expansion schemes, what business was it of mine? Dirk would allow me the space to do the things that were important to me, or I would end our relationship. My spirit was at peace. My heart was doing somersaults. I was my own person. I could walk away. I could let people deal with their problems on their own. I could expand my universe.

I was going to Paris.

On Saturday, I slept late. By the time I got up, Momma Dolly had gone to work. I walked a five-block circuit and ate a big bowl of oatmeal topped with dried cranberries and flax seed and drenched in soy milk.

At the thrift shop I bought a pretty jacket to wear over my black sheath for tonight's dinner with Dirk.

At 6:30 the intercom buzzed. I rode the elevator to the lobby, stepped off, and caught my breath. The sight of Dirk in a dark suit with a pale blue tie, his hair neat and his shoes shined, made me tremble.

He met me halfway across the lobby, took my hands in his and gave a low wolf whistle.

My cheeks felt warm.

The car at the curb was a small Mercedes. He opened the door.

"What happened to your truck?"

Dirk laughed. "I'm not confident enough to drive up to a valet stand at a five-star restaurant in a truck. I borrowed Pop's car."

I got in. He closed the passenger door and got in the driver's side. "Tonight, you choose what to order and then the wine to go with the food."

"I'll need help with the wine. Learning about wine is more complicated than learning how to read a French menu."

"Okay. You select from the wine list, and then I'll give you my opinion if you want me to."

No haughty attitude. No rude remarks. "Thanks, this should be fun."

"A special night," he said. "By the way, you look fantastic."

"Thanks."

ZZZ's was all that I imagined a five-star restaurant

should be. I chose salads and the entrees for us. Dirk nodded his approval. And then I selected a burgundy from the wine menu. Dirk approved and suggested a burgundy from a vineyard and year of equal quality that was several dollars cheaper.

As we ate, Dirk spoke of his progress in getting his parents to expand their business. So far, they'd agreed to buy the building next door, put in a grill and offer a complete breakfast and lunch menu. But franchising and the opening of a second Koenig's bakeshop and restaurant were on hold.

The flow of conversation was easy, the food delicious.

At the end of the meal, Dirk ordered espresso.

The tiny espresso cups with their dark coffee were set in front of us. I breathed in the aroma and took a sip.

Dirk set a box on the table. My heart leaped into my throat. He didn't flip the lid like Herman had, but the box was a ring box. "You don't need to say yes or no right now, Agatha. But, I'm asking you to marry me." Then he opened the box. A ring with a diamond one could see from across the room winked at me.

He sipped his espresso and looked adorable.

"Dirk, I—"

"Think about it while you're gone. When you get back from Paris, you can give me your answer."

"—want to keep my new job. How much travel it involves, I don't know and the job doesn't have regular hours. I have to be available when Mr. Courtney needs me."

I looked down at the table. I wanted to say yes, but I had to be honest with him. I would not give up my job.

Dirk closed the box and put it back in his pocket. He signaled the waiter, paid the check and got up.

I stood. To my surprise, my legs didn't buckle.

Dirk led me out of the restaurant. Neither of us spoke as we waited on the sidewalk for the valet to retrieve the car.

Back in the car, Dirk headed for Millerton. And still, neither of us said a word. The night was dark. The moon and the stars were hidden by clouds. The traffic was sparse.

Halfway to Millerton, Dirk turned the car onto a dark, secluded sideroad and stopped. The next thing I knew, I was in his arms and he was kissing me and I was kissing him back.

Dirk was a right man. And I wanted him to be my right man. But I was no longer willing to ignore my needs for someone else.

After five minutes or so of one long, magnificent kiss, he let go of me and started the car. "Keep your job, Agatha. Stretch your wings. I don't want you to abandon your dream and then later on, when times are dull or difficult, regret your decision."

"Is it possible to have both? Can I travel and work at night when I have to without your resenting my being gone?" I asked as he turned the car into the underground garage of my apartment building.

He didn't answer right away. He parked and came around to open my door. I got out with too much on my mind to worry about being graceful. But instead of starting for the basement door, he wrapped his arms around me and held me for a long time. And then he took a deep breath. "I could, as long as I know you will be coming back to me."

"Always."

Arm in arm we entered the basement. By the light of the glowing furnace and the sound of gurgling pipes, he slipped the ring on my finger.

He took my hand as we headed to my apartment to share the news with Momma Dolly. I opened the door.

Momma Dolly was on the couch nestled next to Mr. Dent. Miss Priss was curled up beside her. TomTom was curled up next to Mr. Dent.

Momma Dolly jumped up. "Agatha, we've been waiting for you to tell you our good news. Mr. Dent and I patched up our differences."

Dirk stepped forward and shook Mr. Dent's hand. He smiled at Momma Dolly. "Congratulations. Agatha and I have good news to share with you. Despite Agatha's misgivings about me, she has agreed to marry me when she gets back from Paris."

Well, I hadn't exactly said when, but why not?

Mr. Dent chortled, got to his feet and was pumping Dirk's hand with vigor. Momma Dolly surrounded us with her arms and squeezed. "I'm so relieved. I'd been worrying about leaving Agatha alone here. If this Mr. Courtney turns out to be a philanderer, I didn't know if she could afford to quit without me helping her with the rent."

Imagine.

I bought my wedding dress in Paris and kept in touch with Dirk through the Internet and by cell phone.

Momma Dolly took charge of making the arrangements for both of our weddings. Dirk's mother and father would be making both wedding cakes. Dirk was consulting with Momma Dolly on the details and phoning last-minute invitations to friends and family. I spent hours wandering around the Louvre and the Orsay Museums ogling the treasures while taking notes about the layout, the collections, and the look, sound and feel of the interiors. Details Mr. Courtney needed for a series of mysteries he planned to write. Each mystery would be set in one of the world's great museums.

I wandered around the Parisian streets, thrilled by the beauty of the old world architecture and by the melody of the conversations in French as I sat at a sidewalk café or when I passed people while strolling through the Tuileries Gardens.

On Friday, Mr. Courtney and I flew home. Dirk picked us up at the airport. We dropped Mr. Courtney off.

And then, with Dirk beside me, I opened the door to my apartment.

Momma Dolly rushed out of her bedroom, wrapped me in her arms, and kissed my cheek. She stepped back and sighed.

"I'm glad you're home safe, Agatha. It's been hectic, but everything's ready for tomorrow. At nine, Herman and I will tie the knot. A brunch will be served after. At three, you and Dirk will be married. And then a reception, with a stunning appetizer table and dancing, will be held."

In her usual manner, Momma Dolly, who didn't believe in wasting time, had planned a full day.

"Thanks for putting everything together. It sounds perfect." I turned to Dirk, gave him a light kiss and sent him home. I went to bed, exhausted and jetlagged.

I woke to the smell of coffee and bacon. Momma Dolly tapped on my door and opened it. "Hurry along, Agatha. We can't be late for my wedding."

She was married wearing a red suit and diamond drop earrings. Miss Priss and TomTom joined the wedding party in separate carriers festooned with flowers.

And then at three, escorted by my mother and my grandmother—who'd changed into a rainbow-colored chiffon dress—I started hitch-stepping down the church aisle to the strains of Mendelssohn played by the church organist.

My chic Paris wedding gown rustled as I moved. In my hands was a bouquet of pink tulips tied with a silvery-pink ribbon.

And standing at the altar, the right man smiled at me.